THE SPARROW

the sparrow

and other stories with poems

by Jane T. Clement
illustrated by Kathy Mow

Plough Publishing House
Rifton, New York

© 1968 by the Plough Publishing House of
The Woodcrest Service Committee, Inc.
Hutterian Society of Brothers
Rifton, NY 12471

First printing   1968
Second printing   1970
Third printing, cloth and paperback   1978

ACKNOWLEDGMENT

The song "The Secret Flower" reprinted by permission
of the Oxford University Press from *The Oxford Book of Carols*.

Library of Congress Cataloging in Publication Data

Clement, Jane T   1917–
    The sparrow, and other stories with poems by
Jane T. Clement. Illustrated by Kathy Mow.
Rifton, N. Y., Plough Pub. House, 1968.
    vii, 198 p. col. illus.
    I. Title.
PZ7.C5902Sp   68-21133
ISBN 0-87486-008-3, cloth
ISBN 0-87486-009-1, paperback

Printed at the Plough Press
Hutterian Society of Brothers
Farmington, PA, USA

CONTENTS

INTRODUCTION

These five stories by Jane Tyson Clement have come out of her experience of life as a member of the Bruderhof, or Hutterian Society of Brothers, where all things are shared in common in the manner of the early Christians.

What these experiences have meant to her will best be expressed by the stories and poems themselves, each with its own unique sense of clarity, longing, and hope. The spirit of each story is given to us visually in the illustrations by Kathleen Fike Mow, who is also a member. She has chosen the scratch-board technique to portray the simplicity and strength of the stories.

The history of the Hutterian Society of Brothers is in itself a fascinating story. This tiny group began to live in Christian community in Germany after World War I. Faced with increasing repressions and then dissolution by Hitler's Gestapo, the Society found a haven in England until World War II forced them to embark on a submarine-threatened voyage to South America. For the next twenty years they were established in three communities in the semi-tropical wilderness of the interior of Paraguay. In 1954 they began a community in the United States, where there was increasing interest in communal living. There are now three communities in the U.S. and one in England. Part of their history is the uniting in basic faith between the Society of Brothers and the Hutterian Church. The latter was first established in the sixteenth century and still today lives communally in the U.S. and Canada.

Introduction

Jane Clement has written the stories in this book out of a full heart, in the spirit of adventure and purpose of this communal life.

In "The King of the Land in the Middle" we have a new fable in which we see ourselves in the self-protective layers of comfortable life, where the coffee should not be "more than enough hot." As the story goes on, the struggle to be fully alive becomes painfully clear.

"The Secret Flower" is the most clearly set in time and place, fourteenth-century England. For this story Jane Clement has done careful research on the historical background, and out of this firm foundation has grown a gripping tale of one man's search for something which has been given different names—the eternal city, the pearl of great price, or the secret flower, sought by each of us and by the whole creation.

The other three stories are bound together by a sense of expectancy, a belief that something new is on the way, a hope that we may be visited by Someone toward whom our longing turns.

There is nothing stilted or moralistic about the figure of this One who comes—the young stranger in "The Sparrow," the tired traveler in "The Innkeeper's Son," and the child in "The Storm." There is rather a sense of earthiness and reality which leaves us with the hope that we also may be found by Him who is seeking us.

Ruby Erickson Moody

THE SPARROW

the sparrow

It was high summer. On the slopes the berry bushes showed the bare nubs where the children had passed through picking, and here and there an unripe cluster still hung, or a few overlooked under the leaves. In the woods the ferns had long since uncurled and the fronds sprang up cool and graceful. The deep greens of summer were misted over here and there in the fields and hedgerows with purple and yellow of phlox and toadflax, the dull white of yarrow and Queen Anne's lace. The hedges were alive with bees in the blossoms, and with the carefree small birds, whose broods were raised. The road to the village of Drury was dusty, as it drove straight through the meadows, curved down a small

3

hill, over the stone bridge, passed along the river valley into the woods, and came out to the cluster of dwellings and shops and the Black Pigeon Inn on the far side.

Just this side of the woods and set a bit back by itself was the cottage of Giles, the wheelwright. It was sturdy but drab, the windows close-curtained and blank, the garden marred by a broken wheel flung down in a flowerbed. Giles hired out to the cartwright in Drury, the most prosperous artisan in the district. Giles was skilled and worth his hire when he was fit to work, but a wearisome man to deal with. Prudence, his wife, swept and scoured, baked and sewed, watched him with a fearful eye, and bent under the weight of discouragement.

His master was a pious man, with his pew in church, and no vices, and was in his way just. But he was as cold and lifeless as a stone. He paid for what he hired, and those who worked for him toed the mark or went home with an empty pocket. He kept Giles because his craftsmanship was high and it paid well to use him in the intervals when he could work. The other times, Giles stalked out of the Black Pigeon and with dark, fearsome face went through the streets of the town, his long legs unsteadily deliberate; and then for a week or more he was seen, now here, now there about the countryside roaming aimlessly, or in a stupor by the river bank, and he would curse all who came near him. While no one came close to him even in his good times, in his bad fits all fled from him, and even Prue, with pinched and stricken face, set his food out upon the stone of the threshold as if he were a wild dog, and watched fearfully to see if he would come to fetch it.

While there is ice at the heart of over-riding loveless-ness, ice and a firm grasp of the ways of this world, with Giles a dark fire burned at the heart of his lovelessness, and the bitter sorrow of the man stung all who brushed past him as if they brushed past nettles. Men said there must be some evil thing in his past which haunted him; or that winter long ago when all his children died of the choking fever had left him weak in the head; but he was never seen in the churchyard near the row of little stones nor was he ever known to speak of them. Unless mumbling or roaring in his drunks he was seldom known to speak at all. It was as if he lived removed from all the comings and goings of men, from the births and deaths, the simple friendships and the lasting loves, the shared hearthfires in the winter, posies picked and brought home by a small hand, songs sung in comrade-ship, shared vigils, shared labor, all the fabric of the common lot. He lived removed also from all pettiness; he did not stoop to try to gain another penny beyond that for which he labored; he cared nothing for what men thought; he had few wants; he never went out of his way, even in his drunken fits, to harm anyone. But all men, good and bad, rich and poor, were cast on the other side of a locked and bolted door. His wife Prue he tolerated merely, as he did the mug he drank from and the cot he slept on. And the glance of his eye or the lift of his hand had such bitterness behind them that the threatened blow was almost felt. He scorned even the rudiments of faith, and at his worst times Prue had even heard him curse God.

So thick and heavy the years of misery had become, Prue could hardly think back to how it had been in the beginning. He was a tall lad, dark with already more than a hint of moodiness. He had come out of the city as an apprentice to her father, and said only that he had no family. She was a quiet little thing, soft-hearted, and eager to mend and comfort, disliking the bold self-confidence of the lads she knew. Her father warned her and refused to help him, sensing a danger in him. But she was caught by his loneliness, and thought somehow to bring merriness into his face, and a free ring to his voice. So they had married and settled in Drury, sought work, and somehow all her hopes had withered. As her little ones died, in her own heaviness she could not ease him, and his darkness drove all fellowship from their door.

When summer fell upon the countryside, sweetening the air with scent and sound, softening the edges of the landscape, filling the days with the labor of field and flock, Prue's heart lifted a bit. From her garden work she would find herself glancing up the road, and if anyone passed she would sit back on her heels to watch, an unaccustomed quiver of hope at her heart, for what she did not know. Or she would leave off stirring the kettle to lean in the doorway, dreaming. But Giles was winterbound all seasons, and really the lovelier the earth the more likely his fits to come upon him.

This summer, as of old, Prue had struggled with the little quiver of hope. In her rare trips to the village she had glanced at each face as if she sought someone. She looked for a sign of friendship, but the stigma of Giles was too strong upon her. She even took a fresh-killed fowl to an ailing woman on the other side of the woods, but the astonished embarrassment of the woman frightened her. "What do they care for us!" she thought. "Even if I gave away everything no one would really care. Men are hard. Only the earth is pure." And she wept a little, out of her dead hopes and weariness.

II
She had wakened that morning before dawn, the old quiver of hope deep within her like the first stirrings

of an unborn child. Restless, she had crept out of bed and hung in the window to watch the east slowly fill with light, the pale curving road emerge, the blackness of the woods recede. To wake before the dawn and watch the day come forth out of creation made that day somehow like a jewel in the hand. Now, mid morning, she knelt in the berry patch, weeding, the sun hot on her back, her fingers stained, her heart bruised, and the wonder and the waiting of the dawn all but drained away. Giles had wakened in a foul mood, and not touching porridge or milk had gone off wordless to his work; the look in his eyes had made her sick half with a hopeless sorrow for him and half with fear. Now in spite of herself and in spite of the years of such mornings, the tears fell on the berry leaves and she wiped her face with her sleeve more than once; and into her mind there crept at last an amazement that still within her there could glow that tiny flicker of hope which was at once her pain and her only joy. She wondered what it could mean, that always it refused to die, to glimmer out, to be quite quenched. For what, for whom, did she hope and wait? Surely for no mortal comfort, no earthly change.

She sank back on her heels, brushing the hair from her eyes, and conscious that over the familiar morning sounds of the little homestead there was a pleasant chatter and stir along the road. Over the rise of the old stone bridge was coming a troop of children, with a tall stranger in the midst of them. They came slowly, evidently listening to a story, at intervals breaking in with comments or laughter. She knew some of them dimly as village children, but others she did not know. Around the troop in circles ran three or four dogs, leaping, coming in to push under the stranger's hand, but never barking. About them all there seemed to gather a brightness lighter than the sunlight, a joyful air, a warmth that refreshed and did not oppress. Prue knelt there transfixed, watching them come, a queer thudding in her breast; she put her hand over her mouth to keep from calling out, though why or what she would have called she did not know. Somehow she felt she must stop them, hold them, receive from them, or join them. They neared the gate, and were passing when a small boy suddenly detached himself from the stranger's side, pushed through the gate, and ran towards her. He carried in his hand a gourd. In front of her he paused with a merry face.

"May I have some fresh water from your well, for the man to drink, if you please?"

Unsteadily Prue rose, took the gourd to the well and filled it, and brought it to the boy. He took it from her hands with a smile, and ran back between the flower-beds to the gate. The troop had paused a moment and now the stranger stopped, taking the gourd. Across the cornflowers and the berry vines he looked at her, and the only sound was the steady hum of bees and the ripple of a wren's song from the lilac bush. The air was luminous and still. Prue stood and took that look, while her heart thudded and a mist swam over her and the palms of her clasped hands came moist and clammy. Then while she watched, tranced, he drank, hung the gourd at his belt, and the troop moved on. Down the road they went and into the woods, singing, and she watched them until they had quite gone, and listened until that last faint golden note had died. But the brightness. . . the brightness had not died!

III

In the cool, new-made morning, with the dew winking on leaf and flower, Giles stood in the door, having woken unrefreshed, sore at heart, time stale within him. The bed of four-o-clocks beside the door with deep green shiny leaves and tight-fisted pink flowers had slung upon it a spider-web unflawed and spangled; it struck at him as he stared at it; again he was engulfed with the useless blank of his own life, the snaggle and snarl of his own self, when a simple low creature could spin such a gem of creation! As Prue came in from the hen house, six white eggs gathered in her apron, he was already on the path, no word or glance for her, the black look on his face, and no breakfast under his belt. Down the road he went, habit taking him to the shop, but within him iron bands tightening, tightening, and the black mood of hate descending.

Once at work he hung over his bench, hardly conscious of the stir and bustle around him. The shop opened directly on the street, the doors flung wide for air and light in the summer warmth. Across the narrow cobbled way was the yard of the Black Pigeon, where urchins flipped stones in the dust. Peddlers came and went, and an old man dozed on a bench in the shade. The casement windows of the inn were wide, the old thick doors set ajar; there was a pleasant sound of voices now and then from within, and the pleasant smell of bean pottage and roasting meat.

As the heat of day increased Giles moved his bench closer to the doors. At the back of the shop there was a great pounding and hammering on the roomy wagon frame for a prosperous farmer of an outlying district. Giles was working on the great wheels, a small pile of finished spokes beside him, and a pile of rough sticks behind him. He picked up a fresh one, secured it, seized the spoke shave, and on the first stroke struck a knot and split the wood. With a curse he flung it on the rubbish pile and as he did so his eye took in the innyard.

The Sparrow

That the pleasant sounds and bustle had had a new note he had been dimly aware. But he was struck now by a curious brightness, as if the sun had shifted. He saw a knot of children and knew the sound had been their laughter and talk. They were gathered around the bench where the old man, now awake, had dozed. A stranger sat there, quite a young man, his face half-hidden by the children but his large deft hands visible as he whittled and worked away at an old piece of wood. Little by little there emerged from the wood a duck, which when finished was handed to the raggedest child. Another gathered scrap of wood was offered and, with much delight from the children, this time a little dog with pointed ears came forth and was seized with eager hands. As the third piece was offered for trans-formation, Giles felt, like a touch of light, the stranger's eyes upon him, and he sullenly shifted back to his work, his heart strangely sore again, the hopeless black like a cloud around him. This time he struck another knot and his thumb slipped and was cut. He cursed again, sucked it, wiped it on his tunic, and labored on. But the wood was flawed, and he flung that away also. The next piece he cut too close. The next piece, with much labor, came right, and was laid on the good pile. He ventured another glance at the stranger, and met a level look that pierced his heart. There was a queer thudding in his breast, the spoke shave clattered from his hand, he rose blindly and stumbled across the cobbles, through the innyard, past the cluster of children who hushed as he went by, the stranger quiet in their midst. Into the dark door he plunged, through the hall, to the bar, where he pounded and shouted for ale.

When he came out, a good hour later, the children and the strange man were gone. Foggy with ale on an empty stomach, uncaring what he did, Giles staggered across the cobbles to the shop, back to his bench. He stopped, swaying, clutching the doorframe. By his bench there lay, instead of a pile of rough sticks, a neat stack of perfect spokes. All the shavings had been swept away, and his spoke shave hung on its accustomed nail. All this Giles took in with swimming eyes, as he stood there, the sound of his own breathing heavy in the still noon air. Then with a curse he wheeled and went off down the road, through the town, out the other way and not towards home. The very dogs cowered away from him as he went, and the good wives shook their heads and clicked their tongues in pity and dismay as they saw him.

Past afternoon, the shadow of the hedges stretched halfway across the road; wren and thrush were silent for awhile in the heat, but a few brown sparrows fluttered their wings in the cool dust where a puddle had long since dried. Giles, who had lain under a bridge for an hour or so in a drunken sleep till roused by the rattle of a wagon over the wooden slats, now wandered back to the road, not knowing or caring which way he went. He carried a stick, the feel of wood in the hand being a habit with him. He walked head down, hunched, aimless. He tried to press from his mind all thought, all feeling, to hold on the merciful blankness in which there was no pain; but the old trick of obliviousness, which had served him in its fashion for so long, could not withstand the little prick of memory, the look of large brown fingers putting the wooden duck into the hands of a dirty child, the pile of spokes by his bench, the brightness in the air of the innyard. Creation around him cried God's praise, the simple deed of love awaited his hand; oh, when had evil drowned him! Where had the wrong road begun with no way back and thick poisonous woods closing in behind! He was the outcast, God's forgotten one!

His hand lifted then, for as if in a dream he saw the sparrow in the dust; the stick flew unerringly; the sparrow fluttered and dropped, a small ruffled heap, its head awry. Giles stopped, staring at what he had done.

Then down the road, in a path of brightness as if out of a cloud's shadow the sun had moved again, he knew someone came. With a terrible effort he looked, and saw that it was the stranger, still far away, coming alone, at a steady pace. With a groan Giles dropped into the deep grass and crawled under the hedge. For a long moment he hid his face, but then as if compelled he raised his head. A queer thudding began in his breast, shaking his frame. Down the road the stranger came; he walked steadily but he saw all that was around him, not like one intent on his own business. The curious brightness hung in the air about him. The thudding grew; Giles could not move except to tremble; his ears began to pound. Nearer came the stranger, and nearer. It was as if all of life hung and trembled in that instant; and in a mist Giles saw the stranger stop, with his eyes on the road. In the dust at his feet lay the dead sparrow. He stooped then, and gathered it up, cupping it against him in his two hands; and Giles, before the pounding in his ears quite overcame him, saw him stretch out his hands and open them; the bird fluttered and hopped upon his fingers, and flew away.

When sense came back to him Giles sat up under the hedge; he felt weak and witless, scarcely knowing his own name. Then in an instant he scrambled up and into the road, searching around in the dust for the dead sparrow; but it was gone. Then he ran first this way and then that way up and down the road but saw no one. He stood there, filling his lungs with air, looking foolish, tears running down his cheeks, the tight bands across his heart parting one by one, the air bright and luminous about him, the cool of evening already stealing out of the wood. Then with a cry of joy he went stumbling across the fields, the quickest way home, to tell Prue.

the Master

He who has come to men
dwells where we cannot tell
 nor sight reveal him,
until the hour has struck
when the small heart does break
 with hunger for him;

those who do merit least,
those whom no tongue does praise
 the first to know him,
and on the face of earth
the poorest village street
 blossoming for him.

bird on the bare branch

Bird on the bare branch,
flinging your frail song
on the bleak air,
tenuous and brave—
like love in a bleak world,
and, like love,
pierced
with everlastingness!

O praise
that we too
may be struck through with light,
may shatter the barren cold
with pure melody
and sing
for Thy sake
till the hills are lit with love
and the deserts flower.

the storm

In a certain village that lay on the banks of a river in the midlands of old England, there lived three brothers. The oldest was the ferryman, the next the miller, and the third the forester of the lord's forest, which bordered the village on the north. So they were all men of some consequence and importance, and were prosperous for those times, having plenty to eat, steady work, tidy houses, and a degree of independence. But the ferryman never sang at his work, as ferrymen are supposed to do, and the miller was not the jolly miller the songs tell us of, so that it was no pleasure to take one's grain to be ground; and the forester tended the beautiful woods with an unseeing and uncaring heart. None had wives

23

to cheer their days, nor dogs to keep them company, nor even a cat to purr on the hearth of a winter evening.

The lord of the fief was a just and temperate man who never taxed unfairly and who lived at peace with his neighbors. But since he was away at the King's Court most of the year he saw to it that he had trust-worthy men as bailiff and steward and warden of his lands. He knew the three brothers and trusted them each one to treat all fairly—the ferryman to charge a fair toll and guard the fishing rights on the river, the miller to keep the fair amount of grain for the lord's granaries and to return the just amount to the people, and the forester to guard the forest well, both timber and wild life, and to deal with poachers with firmness yet with humanity.

So the life of the village went on for a long time, and the three brothers lived from day to day and year to year; their hair greyed a bit and their shoulders grew a little stooped, but they were still hale and strong and did not feel the dampness knotting their knee joints nor their breath growing short when they worked. They never thought about the future or the past but took each day as it came. Once a week on Sundays and on feast days the forester would leave his hut and travel to the mill, and together he and the miller would go by the path along the river to the ferryman, and together the three of them would go wordlessly to church, and after that to the inn to sit in silence over a flagon of ale and venison pie; and then they would go off again, parting with the ferryman first, and then back along the river, where the forester would leave the miller and go on to his solitary, snug hut on the forest's edge.

So it went on, and might have gone on to the end of their days. But they, all unwitting, had not been forgotten, and they, unseeking, yet were being sought for.

For there was a night towards the end of harvest one year when the great storm came. For three days the air had been heavy and dark, and strange white seabirds were seen over the inland meadows, and nights were hushed and dull, the lively crickets silent and the leaves hanging still. The boys who were accustomed to romp on the Common hung about their own cottages, and the little lads and lasses clung to their mothers' skirts in a feeling of nameless fear.

On the third night the tempest descended, first with a whirling of clouds in the upper air, and a soughing in the tree tops, so all fled indoors. And then with the dark came the full fury of wind and rain. The blackness was utter and complete, and each man, no matter how strong, felt his own puniness, and a clutch of fear before the unknown.

Now the forester, during those storm-haunted days, walked through his woods and marked in his mind the dead and dying trees that might topple in a great wind, and he noted how still the beasts were, and how hidden and silent all the birds. He noted the soundness of his little, low, snug hut huddled at the edge of the forest, and was glad that he had built it of stone; but he regretted that he had not long since felled a great dead beech that stood a hundred yards from his door.

So it was that the night the storm broke he sat within, the dim glow of the embers on his hearth and the light of one candle on the table throwing shadows that veered and flickered on the walls. He crouched in fear and dread, listening to the tumult without; and he thought of his trees, and the beasts of the forest who would find little shelter, and he thought of his brothers and how they were faring, and at length he thought of the people of his village, in their flimsy cottages, with their meagre harvest unprotected. A little surge of pity crept into his heart; and in that instant he heard the child crying.

At first he did not know what it was he heard, over the howling of the wind and the pounding of the rain. But then it came again, faint and clear—the crying of a child. He rose and went to the door and stood with his hand on the latch.

"I cannot go out there," he thought. "I would be blown away, or crushed beneath a falling limb. I am an old man. And what child would be abroad now? Have I lost my wits?"

But even as he whispered to himself, the cry came again; and after it there was a great crash, the long, thundering roar of a tree falling, and he knew the

great beech had gone. He waited, frozen, straining his
ears, but no further cry came. Then he waited no longer,
but flung open the door, pulling it to behind him, and
plunged into the tempest in the direction of the fallen
tree; through the raging dark he went, gasping and
struggling, until he ran into the sprawling branches.
Then on his knees he crawled, feeling with his hands
along the ground, under the great prostrate trunk, and
calling, "Little one, little one! Where are you? I am here
to help! Little one, answer me!"

After an agony of searching, his hands felt a small,
wet face, and his palm felt the fluttering beat of a small
heart. The child lay pinned under a limb. He began to
pull and tug at the limb, and taking his knife from his
belt he began to hack away, gently easing the little body
free as he worked. It was as if a strange glow surrounded
him, for he could see in the dark; and as he slid the little
one free, and gathered him up in his arms, the path lay
clear before him, and the wind seemed to still and
the rain to slacken before his feet.

So he carried the child home in safety, and once
within doors, he laid him by the hearth, hastening to
blow on the embers and freshen the fire. He stripped
the wet boy, wrapped him in his cloak, and he chafed
his cold hands and feet. He looked him all over tenderly
for any broken bones, and carefully wiped the blood
away from a long scratch that lay across his brow. At
length the child sighed and woke; he stirred and looked

about him, and then smiled into the face of the forester. And with that smile the wind seemed to die away, the drumming of the rain ceased, and a peace fell on the world.

Then the child turned over and snuggled on his side in the old cloak, and fell asleep. The forester watched by him, gazing on the small, still face, the tangled hair, and the little brown hands, until in exhaustion of body and soul he too slumbered.

He awoke to a blaze of sunlight and the singing of birds; his door was flung wide and the cool morning wind flowed in. The hearth was empty, save for his old cloak and the bloodstained rag. The little tattered clothes that had been hung to dry were gone, and the child had vanished. He rushed to the door, calling out into the new morning: "Little one, little one! Where are

you?" But it was the birds that answered, and the squirrels running about on the fallen trees, and the rabbits leaping in the grass.

Then he looked on the devastation of his forest, and he thought of his brothers and the people of his village, and a great pity surged into his heart, and a joy that he was still alive to help them. And he rushed off down the path.

Now the miller had worked in a fever during those dark days to gather in the grain, till all the lord's harvest was stored safely in the great stone mill. The night the storm descended he climbed into his bed early, pulled the cover over his head to shut out the noise of the tempest and the raging river, prayed that the tiles would not fly off his roof, and sank into a restless slumber. Then he dreamed he was a boy again, playing in the meadow with his brothers, and he dreamed that in anger he struck his younger brother and flung him in the grass, where he lay in a heap and cried pitifully. And in his dream he felt in his heart a tinge of remorse for the loveless blow he had dealt his small brother. And in that instant he awoke, and heard indeed a child crying, over the tumult of the storm.

He lay huddled in his warm bed listening, and a tumult arose in his heart. What was he to do, an old man? Risk his limbs in such a storm? And what child would be abroad in such a night? Had he lost his wits? But then the crying came again, pitiful and weak, and smote his heart anew. So he rose and rushed to his door. The wind buffeted against it and the rain poured in torrents, but he pushed it open and let it slam to behind him. Then in the wild dark he listened for the cry, and it came again, down the path; and on his knees so that he could feel his way he crawled, calling out, "Little one, little one, I am coming! Do not fear. I am coming." And at length, when his knees were torn and aching, and his hands bruised, and his voice hoarse with calling, he found a rock by the path and clinging to it a little huddled form, sobbing and sobbing. At the touch of his hands the small arms went around him, the wet wild head was on his shoulder, and he felt the sobs that shook the pitiful frame. "Never fear, little one, you are safe," he crooned, and rose to his feet, for the path was strangely clear now, and the wind and rain ceased to buffet him. So he carried the boy safely home, and once in, laid him tenderly on his bed, stripped off his wet clothes, and wrapped him in his blanket. He carefully wiped the blood from a long thorn-scratch that lay across the little boy's brow, then he brought him broth to sip; the child sat with his head against the miller's shoulder, gradually his sobs ceased and his breath that had come in shuddering gasps came evenly again. Then he looked into the miller's face and smiled, and with that smile the sound of the wind died away, and the rain passed, and a peace fell on the world. Then the child lay down, and snuggled in the blanket to sleep. The miller watched by his side for a long time, and then lay down on his own hearth, with his cloak rolled up under his head, and slept, out of his exhaustion of body and soul.

When he awoke the door stood wide, and the sunlight of all the world streamed in; the birds sang in the fresh, new-made morning. The miller leapt up and rushed to the bed, but the child had vanished; the little garments hung up to dry were gone; there was nothing but the imprint of his form on the bed, and a bloodstained rag, and an empty cup. Then he ran to the door and cried, "Little one, little one, where are you?" But the only answer was the song of the bird. Then he saw the devastation of the storm, and he thought of the flattened and ruined grain of the villagers, and the fat harvest that had been gathered safe in his mill, and a great pity filled his heart. And he saw the path before him, the path to the village, and he set off at a run, with strong hands and a newly-beating heart, to serve.

The ferryman had grumbled for days. The river had been running wild and sullen and dark, almost at flood crest, and he had pulled his ferry far up the bank and lashed it to the stoutest trees. Then for no amount of money would he take any across. He sat on his doorstep and studied the sky and counted his losses and felt sour and discontent. The night the storm descended, he went indoors early, bolted the heavy shutters, and sat over a flagon of beer, listening to the roar of the river and the wild wind, and the beating of the rain.

He thought of his brothers and wondered how they were faring, if they were safe as he. Then he thought of the village and the peasants with their little fields now being beaten and pummeled. And he remembered the man and his wife who had stood on the far bank but yesterday and called to him to fetch them across, for they had been to the town to a wedding, and now wished to get home to their children before the foul weather broke. But he in hardheartedness had not heeded them and had gone inside, and at length they had gone away, up river. With a pang he wondered where they were, and how their children fared; in his heart he felt a stir of remorse that he had been so cold and hard and careful for his own skin. And in that instant he heard a child crying.

He set his flagon down and listened, straining his ears, and again the cry came. He leapt to his feet in terror then, for indeed the cry came, not from near at hand, but borne by the wind from across the water, from the far bank. He stood rooted to his floor thinking, "What cry is this? What child is abroad on such a night? Am I, an old man, to risk all, crossing the river on such a night? Impossible! I cannot! I would be out of my wits!" But the cry came again, desperate and clear. He stood, in his heart a battleground, then he pounded with his fist on the table and shouted, "Fool that I am!" and rushed out into the wild and roaring dark.

In the swirl and tumult he pressed his way to the bank and stood waiting for the cry again, and when it came he judged its source—down river near the bend; it came thin and clear and lost. He strained his eyes staring into the pitchy dark, and then as if the moon glowed for an instant through the flying clouds he caught the faintest glimmer of a small form, downstream, clinging to the overhanging willow near the bend.

"Blessed God," he gasped, "the little one will be drowned if I do not hasten."

Up the bank he plunged then, to where the ferry was securely tied. In the dark his fingers struggled with the ropes and freed them one by one, then he dragged the ferry down the bank, pushing it into the raging river, and leaping aboard, pole in hand. Down the

rushing torrent he was borne, thrusting in his pole to ease the tossing craft across the river if he could; as he poled he gave thanks each time he felt the sturdy pole strike the bottom, and he shouted, "Little one, hold on! Little one, I am coming!" His shoulders ached, his chest burned, and his breath came in gasps; he struggled to keep on his feet, and to keep the pole in his hands. But he would not give up, and a final lunge took him against the far bank, where the ferry caught in a snag and swung round beneath the willow; he caught the body of the child; the little arms let go and the child dropped down fainting. The ferryman sat on the slippery, rocking deck of his ferry with the rescued boy in his arms and he wept, for joy and relief and exhaustion. The weeping hurt him, so unaccustomed was it to him, who had not wept since childhood; the tears rained down on the little white face that lay against his breast, and the child stirred and woke from his swoon. He looked up in amazement and then he smiled into the eyes of the ferryman. And with that smile the wild wind died away, and the rain ceased, faint stars shone through the clouds, and the ferry rested peacefully on a quiet river.

"Now to get thee home, little one," breathed the ferryman. "The river is at peace, by some miracle, and there is such a glow in the sky that I can see the way easily." He laid the child gently on the deck and seized the pole again, thrusting the craft off from the shore, and with sure strokes pushing across stream till they lodged on the bank. Then he stooped and gathered up the wet and shivering child, hurried up the bank and carried the light body home.

There he laid him on a pallet by the fire and stripped him of his wet clothes, wrapped him in his warm cloak, and tenderly wiped away the streak of blood from a long scratch across his brow. The child slept quietly then, and the ferryman knelt by his side for a long while, gazing into his face. Then at length he sighed and became aware of his own aching weariness; he sank down on his cot, and slept.

When he woke the door stood open wide, the sunlight of a new morning flooded in, he heard the kingfisher calling over the river and the singing of a lark. He leapt up then and ran to the hearth, but the child had vanished. By the pallet lay the bloodstained rag with which he had cleaned the wound. The little garments that had been hung to dry were gone. He ran to the doorway then and cried aloud to the new day, "Little one, little one, where are you?" But nothing answered. The ducks paddled peaceably in a little backwater by the shore, and the kingfisher on the far bank rattled. He stood looking at the devastation of the storm, his ruined garden, the broken trees. He thought then of his brothers, if they were still alive, and of the stricken village, and his heart ached for them all. But he looked at his hands, hard and strong and able, and he thanked

God for them; then he set off down the path to the village, his heart filled only with a desire to serve. And as he went he looked up, to see his brothers coming, such a light on their faces as he had never seen before.

On the path they met and stood looking at one another. Wordlessly they clasped hands. The forester was the first to speak. "In the night, brother, I heard a child crying, and I found him."

And the miller broke in, "And I also, brother."

And the ferryman cried aloud, "And I also, my brothers. On the far bank he was, nearly to drown, but I reached him in time...and when he smiled the tempest died...and this morning he was gone."

"Even so it was with us," the miller said. And the three stood silent, filled with wonder. After a long while the forester spoke. "And now the world is newly made." Then together they turned and went off to the village to see how they could serve.

The great storm had indeed left ruin in its wake, and death to man and beast. Three had died, one a little girl who had strayed seeking her lost kitten, one an old man whose heart had stopped from fear, and one a young husband who had been killed in the falling of a tree. Houses were broken, fruit trees down, flocks and herds scattered, fields laid waste. But wherever the brothers went sorrow was eased, a new hope came, warmth crept into the heart. At length they all rallied; what little was left was shared freely. Together they mourned and buried their dead, together they began to rebuild.

The three went to the lord of the fief and laid before him their need.

"There is grain in the mill but none for the villagers," said the miller.

"There is firewood and game aplenty in the forest, but cold hearths and no food in the cottages," said the forester.

"There is plenty of fish in the river, but not to be had by right," said the ferryman.

And the lord of the fief could not withstand the light in their faces. "The forest, the river, and the mill belong to the village now," he said. "I have no need of them."

So they all lived through the first hard winter, which was indeed the most joyful they had ever known.

And thenceforth the miller sang at his work, and the children begged to be allowed to carry the grain to the mill. The forester always had a child at his side as he walked through his woods and together they discovered the nests of the birds, and the dens of the foxes, and the thickets where the shy deer hid, and each tree became a friend. And the ferryman took children back and forth across the river all day for the price of a song, so that the river rang with their music and their laughter. And all people shared what they had; none went hungry or cold or suffered loneliness and fear; and this they did out of their new joy, and because it was like a new morning.

And strangers coming to that village were puzzled, feeling something had been won in that place; for it was different from all other places they had seen. And the villagers could only say, "It was the Great Storm, when we suffered so much. Then this joy came to us, and the world was new made."

And the brothers kept the Child in their hearts.

february thaw

On the wet bank's rim we stand,
the air wild with the beating rain;
the sodden wood beyond awry
with wild wind from the driven sky:
    (and I know deeply and with pain
      we stand here once but not again.)

The crumbling, heaving thrust of ice,
the thundering tumult of the falls,
familiar crisis of the year,
the swift blood beating in the ear:
    (but only once, within the heart
      the ice piles ready to depart.)

The men are knotted by the dam,
the grinding floes rear up and roar
and press and push; and with a shout
we watch the jam come tumbling out:
    (so may we shout, so may we sing,
      O blessed thaw, O holy spring!)

song of the convert

Stand still, my heart, and praise
the hills that round you lie;
stop here, my soul, and raise
joy to the circling sky!

All ruin that befalls,
all pain that twists and mars,
drowns not the voice that calls,
leaves on God's life no scars.

Then lift your jubilee
and never cease to sing!
this day all men are free
who kneel before the King!

the innkeeper's son

It was a bitter night, though very clear. Under the sparkling stars a wild north wind drove cold into the veins, into the cracks and crannies of the tightest dwelling, and the tree limbs sighed and creaked. The snow that had fallen yesterday swirled up afresh and made new drifts, and the frozen earth was swept bare in wide swathes. No creature moved abroad, and except for the moan of the wind the world lay silent.

But the inn was warm and cosy in the firelight and in the lamplight flickering from the walls. The smell of roast goose and pudding and spiced wine permeated the air. There was the glitter of holly on the shelf above the hearth, and greens were hung in bunches from the great black rafters. The four men at the table set their flagons down in unison with loud thumps and burst into raucous singing, not for the first time that evening to be sure.

> "God rest you merry, gentlemen,
> Let nothing you dismay,
> For Jesus Christ our Saviour
> Was born upon this day!"

Perhaps it was concern for the decorum of his house that brought the innkeeper from the kitchen then—or perhaps concern for a sale of more ale—for he came in bearing a foaming jug and set it before them, and stood with arms akimbo, grinning, as they filled their mugs and drank his health. Then his glance flickered to the settle by the hearth, where his boy sat alone. He was a slender lad, dark, with great blue eyes that stared emptily into space, blinking occasionally. His hands lay upon his knees. The innkeeper's face shadowed a moment, then his mind came back to his guests.

"So, gentlemen, here is more cheer for you this bitter eve. The goodwife sends you greetings, and hopes you won't tarry too long this night from your own hearths."

The townsmen laughed and the first one spoke, "More cheer here than on my own hearth! Bickerings and brawling brats! No peace on earth for a man there, Christmas Eve or no!"

But the second chided him. "Come now, what say

you, Nat! They are all hale and hearty, just a bit lively and numerous! This is a holy eve, and like as not we should all be home!" and he pushed back his chair as if to rise. But the third laid a hand on his sleeve, saying, "Like as not, but it's warm and merry here, and cold and bleak without."

And in a low voice the last one spoke, "But a night of mystery all the same. We should be home by our own hearths, for this is the night the Christ Child walks, by the old legends."

Then the innkeeper leaned upon the table with his hands and shook his head. "A likely tale, a likely tale!"

"Nay, but 'tis true!" broke in the second. "You know the kindly woodcarver from Terminaison beyond the mountain who said a heavenly visitor carved him a most marvelous chest when he was an awkward and mistreated lad?"

And the third spoke, remembering, "And that woman of the same town whose long-lost husband was led home by a fair-haired angel child one Christmas Eve, after years of wandering?"

"And that lame girl," said the fourth man. "Do you recall that lame girl in the next village—the village of La-Croche—she who gave her last crust to a little lost boy—and next morning awoke with legs as strong and straight as yours or mine?"

Then the innkeeper glanced again at his son on the settle by the hearth, and he eased himself onto a stool

47

and put his head close to his guests. "There was a time," he said in a low voice, "when I prayed for him, yonder, that his affliction would be lifted. Aye, and my wife and I laid many pence before the altar, and lit many a candle. But his eyes are still vacant, and scant use a blind lad is to a man like me! He does what he can, but that is little enough."

But the boy had heard, for he drooped his head and passed one hand across his eyes. Then he sat as before. A little silence fell upon the room, and the fire crackled and hissed. At length the first townsman spoke.

"Such tales are told to give us comfort. Not one of us has seen such with our own eyes. 'Tis true that now Terminaison has a name for good works that is unsurpassed in all the province, and the girl in La-Croche is said to be a veritable saint, giving of her own to the poor till there is nothing left for herself. But who can say the world itself has changed?"

Still the uneasy silence lay upon the room. The boy sat with bowed head, the innkeeper poked at the fire, and the men slouched in their chairs, all merriment quenched. Then the third townsman slapped his thigh and spoke in a loud voice.

"The priests sometimes, to get our pence and our candles, spread these miracles. I do right as I see it, and look for no sudden and unearned ending to my troubles. But nay, nay, why be sad, for the world is full of sorrows and disappointment, if we dwell upon it!" And he rose with the jug, to lean across the table and fill all their mugs, until the last drop was drained.

So they all broke into song again, and as they sang they did not hear the soft knock, nor see the latch move and the door slowly open. The stranger stood against the night unnoticed, watching them; then he quietly shut the door behind him. He was dark and thin, and wore a threadbare cloak, and clutched a gnarled staff with one brown hand. He waited for a moment while their song rang out.

> "In Bethlehem in Jewry
> This blessed babe was born
> And laid within a manger
> Upon this blessed morn."

But the boy had turned his head with the opening of the door, and rose now, his hand against his heart and his head following the stranger as he slowly crossed to the fire, laid down his staff, and stretched out his hands to the warming flames. And suddenly the song died out, as the innkeeper saw the newcomer by the hearth and got to his feet, with a troubled face.

"What now, a wayfarer, on such a night! What do you seek, stranger?"

But the man simply looked up, smiling, and held his brown hands to the flames. The innkeeper, a bit nettled, said grudgingly, "Well, warm yourself, and later I'll fetch you a bite. 'Tis no night to turn a man out!" Then to the four silenced townsmen, "So now,

lads, 'tis going on twelve o'clock, and like it or not soon
out ye go!"

And they all chimed in:

"One more toast, that this blessed eve is a bright
one the world around!"

"Riches, and a long life!"

"Health, and an obedient wife!"

"An end to all domestic strife!"

They drained their tankards and banged them down
with loud laughing and crowded to the door, flinging
sheepskin jackets over their shoulders, slapping one
another upon the back. The innkeeper followed them,
herding them out like noisy and unruly cattle. He shut
the door upon them, calling cheerily, "God bless you
one and all, and until next year!" and they were heard
going off into the night with shouts and singing.

In the silence that fell the innkeeper stood a moment,
his face blank and tired. Then he came wearily back
to the table, gathering up the empty tankards and the
soiled cloth. On his way to the kitchen door he stopped
a moment, looking to the fire where the man still stood,
and to his son, who waited in the shadow.

"Son, fetch this stranger the ends of bread from the
pantry, and see that he is well-warmed before he goes
forth. I'm off to bed. Tomorrow bids fair to be a busy
one, and my bones ache." Then he went across the
room, kicking the door open with his toe and letting it
fall to behind him.

After a long moment, when the fire whispered and glowed more golden and peace seemed to come gathering down from the shadowing corners, the man gave a vast and weary sigh. He sank upon a low stool by the fire and laid aside his cloak. He felt his worn shoes, now thawing and wet, and slipped them off to set them nearer the flames to dry. The boy still stood with his face toward the man, but now he turned and went to the hutch. He felt carefully around till he found the snowy cloth covering six loaves of fresh, white bread. One of these he drew forth and laid it on the board, cutting it in generous slices. These he put on a wooden trencher, and then fetched a wedge of yellow cheese from the shelf. Slowly he crossed the room and set the supper on a bench beside the stranger. For a long moment the man looked up into the boy's face, glowing in the firelight; then he began to eat. Again the boy turned and crossed the room, and this time he brought back a slender green bottle of mead, and a blue mug. These he set down beside the bread and cheese. He stood for a moment, as if listening to be sure the man was indeed eating, then he went to the great chest in the corner of the room. Opening this, he lifted from it a fur rug. He carried the rug back to the fire and kneeling, spread it carefully before the hearth. Then he rose and backed off and spoke softly, "Master, when thou art done, rest awhile."

He slipped away then into the shadows and sat on a

stool, waiting. When the man had finished, he stretched out on the rug in the warmth of the flickering fire and sighed again, and after a bit there came the sound of peaceful breathing. Then the boy arose and felt his way carefully across the room. He stooped over the man, and with his hands hunted for the shoes laid out to dry. With his delicate fingers he felt the soles and found the holes in them; then he laid them against his own foot, to try to size. The match was perfect. He slipped off his own shoes and put them where the man's had been. Then he went back across the room and set the old shoes beside the great chest. From a peg on the wall he took down a cloak, his own, heavy and serviceable. He crept back across the room and felt again on the floor near the man, until he found his cloak. He ran his fingers over the worn spots, the patches, and the holes. Then he laid his own cloak down in its place, and took the old one back across the room, putting it on the peg where his had been. Then he went softly across to the settle near the hearth and sank upon it, and he whispered to himself, "I will watch by his side tonight, lest he lack for anything."

The clock struck the hour of one, and the man slept on. The boy sat unwavering, his face peaceful and full of joy. The quiet room was bright with the steady glow of firelight, for the wood seemed not to be consumed, though no seen hand replenished it. The sound of the wind faded, and the hiss of blown snow against the

pane. The flicker of starlight came beyond the window.

The clock struck the hour of two, then three, then four, and still the man slept, and the boy, smiling faintly, watched on. But then the peace, the utter quiet and content, settled over his heart and little by little his head nodded, till his cheek rested against the side of the settle, and his blind eyes closed.

When the clock struck five, the man stirred. He stretched, and then sat up, and in the faint, warm light he took in the sleeping boy, the new shoes, the sturdy cloak. He rose then, and in the old room he seemed very tall and fair, a king and not a beggar from the road. He swung the cloak about his shoulders and slipped his feet into the shoes, and knelt to fasten them. Then he crossed the room and stood for a long moment looking into the face of the boy. He reached out his hand and with one finger he softly touched the eyelids of the boy, and then with gentleness he stroked his hair. The boy smiled in his sleep but did not waken. Then the man turned and went across the room to the door. The latch clicked as the door swung wide, a gust of morning air, cool and fresh, blew in, and then without a sound the door closed. On the hearth the fire suddenly winked down, only a few coals glowing still, and the room grew chill.

Perhaps it was the chill that woke the boy, or in his heart the knowledge that a presence was gone. For he suddenly jerked awake, and with wide eyes looked into the dim room, where dawn was already striking at the windows. He stared, leapt to his feet and rushed to the hearth.

"Master!" he cried. "Thou art gone! I slept! I did not watch by thee!" And he bent his head upon his knees, and wept. But then his sobs suddenly ceased. He raised his head and took his hands from his eyes and looked around.

"But I see!" he gasped. "I see!" He seized the crust of bread left upon the trencher and the crumbs of cheese. "Look, where he ate!" And he felt the fur robe with wondering fingers. "And see where he has lain." Then he saw the staff. "And this, this he leaned upon." He leapt up then, holding the old staff, and ran to the chest in the corner. "And these are his shoes, and this his cloak. Here are the rents I felt last night . . . but now I see . . . I see!" He stood dumbstruck, panting, and stared around the room, the tears upon his cheeks. "But oh where, where has he gone!" Then he rushed to the door and flung it wide and looked out upon the world. He stood thus, clutching the frame, while the blue and rose and gold of the first dawn grew and blossomed in the east. "Oh praise, oh praise," he gasped, "for such beauty! O praise to Him forevermore!"

"Hast lost thy wits, stupid boy!" thundered his father, in the dark, cold room behind him. "Shut the door! Put wood upon the fire and hasten. This day ye know full well the draper and all his clan feasts here.

'Tis Christmas and more to do than we have hands to manage. Shut the door, thou fool!" He pulled the boy back and slammed the door to in a fury. "Now the room is icy. We must start the fire afresh before we set up the trestles and lay the cloth. Look lively! Nay, I wonder at thee!"

He went to the bin behind the settle and brought out a log, lugging it to the hearth. In the shadows he stumbled over the fur rug and with a tinkle of glass the bottle of mead toppled over and smashed. The innkeeper dropped the log and stared about him in dismay, and with an oath turned to face his son. The boy stood staring at him with wide, dark eyes, his face stricken.

"Is this the way ye served that beggar last night? Mead!" He nudged the trencher with his foot. "White bread! The best robe! Are ye bewitched, crazed?"

The boy stood, wordless. Then the father went up and seized him by the shoulder. "Fool, blind fool," he shouted into his face. "Without sight and without wit also! What have I done to deserve such misfortune!" He gave him a shove, then, in a calmer voice—"Fetch kindling from the bin and stir the fire. And don't cut thy stupid knees on that glass. I'll get the broom to sweep it up. The next stranger that comes I'll deal with myself, and give him short shrift!" And he went out muttering into the kitchen.

The boy looked after him, his face pale, the tears

welling out of his eyes. For a long moment he stood, trembling, the silence of the empty room pounding in his ears. He raised his hands and pressed them over his eyes, and whispered: "Oh, Master, who has given me sight, now I must serve thee, and follow thee, even to the ends of the earth. But where, where has he gone!"

Then he lifted his head, listening. Words came back to him, spoken half in disbelief, yet with a core of truth. "La-Croche," he whispered. "Terminaison...perhaps there. At least I would find others who have seen him also, and believed."

He went across the room. With sure and steady hand he took the stranger's shoes and put them on his own feet. He flung the man's cloak across his shoulders, and he held the old staff in his hands. Then without a backward glance he strode to the door, opened it, and disappeared into the morning, and the door swung shut behind him.

the chain

Too late we break the siege
of the close-bastioned heart,
and find the city starved,
dry to the bone, and dark.

Too late we cut the chain
who cannot find the key;
the captive soul has died,
the captive flame is quenched.

The Devil does not thrust
against the armored gate;
nor counsels us to yield—
he counsels us to "wait".

the king of the and in the middle

Once upon a time, not so long ago but that the dragons had already become legendary and the last unicorn had vanished into the forests, and one could no longer go into the world to seek one's fortune with some likelihood of finding it, there was a king of a certain kingdom. Now this kingdom was neither North nor South, East nor West, but more or less in the middle of things. And this king was neither tall nor short, dark nor fair, thin nor stout, wise nor foolish, wicked nor good, but just about middling in all of these qualities. He had about the ordinary amount of courage, humor, agility, intelligence, greed, unselfishness, and anything else one might think of.

Now this was a period in the childhood of the world

when the time of fairy tales was drawing imperceptibly to a close. If we are living in a time of change we seldom know it—unless we are extraordinarily wise and gifted, as this king was not. It is only later, when the path already trod is all laid out behind us, that the historians look back and nod their heads sagely, and set names to this stretch or that. When this king lived, the kind of magic the fairy tales tell us of had all but faded away—no touch of a wand could transform a loathsome frog into a handsome prince, no secret chant open an unknown cave in a mountainside where treasure gleamed. What spells there were, were of a more subtle nature, and treasure could go unrecognized.

Our king had a pleasant castle, with no luxury but no discomfort either, set on a middling-sized out-cropping of rock by a middling-sized river, across from which lay pleasant and adequate fields.These yielded him a decent living, along with all his people. There was also a nice, comfortable amount of mineral deposits in the neighborhood, to be mined by comfortably-paid miners who delved into the hillsides with a minimum of danger or discomfort.

The king had a pleasant-enough wife and four sturdy children, two of each kind, not exceptionally bright or dull, naughty or good. They lived a bit aloof from the other folk of that little land, as was right and proper. There were no great feasts, as nothing happened to celebrate. Birthdays were everyday affairs, and death, when it visited, came at the end of one's period of "usefulness." Life was so well-ordered and calm none grew weary before their time or bent under stress and died too young; disease was scarcely known, so held no fear. Winters were mild and pleasant. Spring came gradually and in no glorious burst. Summers were warm and long but never hot, and autumn was a gradual fading away into the first snowfalls. Of wild and dangerous beasts there were none, only the harmless rabbit and here and there a herd of brown deer. The birds that flitted in the hedges had soft colors and pleasant songs but nothing that stopped one's breath and held one wonder-struck. The flowers were plentiful but mild of hue, and the bees were busy as usual but not frantic and dizzy with the ravishing scent and sight of blossoms, and so unmolested they had quite forgotten how to sting.

So little happened that there was no history in the schools, and sums were so simple as to be no pain to anyone even had there been an exceptionally dull scholar (which of course there was not). There were no ballads, since there was no history to sing of, and no odes, as there was nothing to write them about, and no elegies, as there was no great sorrow, and no songs of praise, for what could be praised in that unexceptional, peaceful existence?

Now it so happened, one spring morning, that the king awoke at his usual time, seven o'clock or so, and in due course rang his little bell for breakfast. Breakfast was always a beaker of fresh milk, two eggs, two rolls, and a mug of coffee. The page brought it all in on a tray, set it before the king, bowed, and retired. And the king, as usual, took up his coffee first of all for a swallow or two.

Then, for the first time in his experience, an extraordinary thing happened. The coffee was boiling hot! He spat out his swallow and sat gasping, with his mouth open, fanning his burning tongue, his eyes watering, and a most peculiar feeling creeping all over him. He had wits enough soon to take a long drink of cool milk, and then he sat back, staring before him out of the window over the green fields, this same queer feeling tingling at the roots of his hair and curling along his spine. There was no word for that feeling in their language, since there had been no need for it, but we know it as —astonishment.

The king sat there, filled with astonishment. Something was the matter with his coffee. And then into his mind crept another feeling, a pushing little feeling that left him restless. It was, if he could have put a word to it, curiosity. *What* was the matter with his coffee, and why?

At last, when he had sat still for a while and aired his sore tongue, he slowly reached out his hand again to his little bell, and rang. The page below, in the kitchen, felt a little quiver of something (astonishment, we know it to be) when he heard the king's bell so soon again, but up he went and before his monarch, who simply looked at him and said:

"Who prepared the coffee this morning?"

"A lad came in from the highway yesterday, sire, and asked for a night's lodging, and said he would pay for it in labor. Steward didn't know what to say so said yes. He helped Cook this morning and fixed the coffee, sire."

"He fixed it all right," said the king, feeling his sore tongue. "What did he do to it?"

The page wasn't used to questions and didn't know what to say. He stammered, for once at a loss for words.

"I—I don't know, sire. What was wrong with it?"

The king sat and thought. What was wrong with it, anyway? At last he said, "It was more than enough hot."

"Oh," said the page, who had never heard of such a thing.

"Where did the lad come from?"

"I do not know, sire. He came by on the highway."

There was another puzzled silence. Finally the king spoke again, and who's to say what event was more fateful for him, the coming of the strange lad to the kitchen, the swallow of the boiling coffee, or the next words he spoke:

"Send him in to me."

And so the lad came before the king, and again the king felt the tingle in his hair and the pushing questions in his mind as he looked at him; for the lad was very tall, and dressed in bright green, with a brooch like a dark green leaf fastening his tunic. He had black hair and a lively eye, and he looked at the king with a smile.

"You asked for me, sire?"

"Yes." And they looked at each other.

At last the lad said, "What did you wish of me, sire?"

"You fixed my coffee this morning?" and the king gestured to the tray still before him.

"Yes, sire, I was so privileged. What was amiss with it?"

The king frowned, hunting for the right word to express it.

"It was more than enough hot."

"Too hot, was it too hot?" Then the lad slapped his thigh and laughed. "Is that all, sire? A thousand pardons! In my land we like it so hot it warms one all the way down to the toes and to the tips of the ears! On a frigid winter morning when the gale is blowing in great blasts and snow drives in the cracks of the windows, what gives a man courage like a mug of coffee right off the fire! On a mild spring morning like this I should have used my wits and been more temperate!"

Then the king sat and stared with his mouth open, and not for a burning tongue. Such gales and snows he'd never heard of, and to be warmed to the tips of one's ears! And what did the word "temperate" mean to one who had not known extremes?

66

"Where did you come from?" he managed at last to say.

The lad put one foot up comfortably on a bench then, and rested his elbow on his knee.

"Away up North," he said. "I'm a forester. Our ancient maples have a blight. Some leaves curl and drop before the flaming fall comes, and branches die here and there. We dared not tap the trees for their sweet sap for three seasons now for fear of weakening them, and we lack sugar badly. I'm traveling South to where there are great forests, to seek out those foresters and learn if they know of such a blight, and its cure. They are noble trees, and make all the land golden before the winter storms break. They nourish us in our need, and shade us from the blazing summer suns. If they can be saved, we would like to know. I saw no such trees hereabouts, sire. Do you not know them?"

"No," said the king, faintly. "I know them not."

"I saw no peach trees, either—orchards that lie pink and fragrant in the spring, and the bees go fair wild with it, and one can scarce get to one's work with gazing! Spring comes late in our land, later than here— but it seems more fair. I know not..." and he looked out the window in a puzzled way, "this land seems lackluster, lifeless." He looked back at the king. "Nor have I heard any singing, only a tuneless humming now and then. Is the land in mourning? I saw no signs of grief. But no joy, either."

67

"No," said the king. "For what would we mourn? Why should we sing?"

The forester straightened up then and looked at the king a long moment. Then he sat down on the bench and leaned forward earnestly.

"Did you never lose anyone by death?"

"My mother, and my father. But they were growing old, and I was grown, and their time had come."

"Were you never given children, sire, to bring grace to your days?"

"Yes, two sons and two daughters."

"Did you never lose a child, a little one?"

"No. I do not remember such a happening in all the kingdom."

"Truly you have been blessed," said the forester in a hushed voice. Then after a little silence, "My small sister died, two years old, as bright and lovely as a meadowlark—gone, just like that. When we laid her away my mother's heart near broke with grief. Her greatest joy now is to tend all the sick ones in the village, and if death comes, the first one turned to is my mother, so steadfast is her courage now. And no one rejoices more in the children that are given! Truly one must suffer loss to know what it is to receive a gift!"

The king put his elbows on the table and his head in his hands. His ears seemed to pound and his wits seemed scattered. He closed his eyes and felt his world whirling. The silence deepened between them, and then the lad jumped up.

"I rattle on too much, sire! I am always told I talk too much! Forgive me. I tire you, and keep you from your labors for your kingdom, and tell you all about myself, and your breakfast sits there, and your coffee cools. But it was too hot, remember, which was why you summoned me. I'll run fetch another cup now, which shall be neither hot nor cold . . ." and he made to leave.

"Stay," said the king. "Sit please, and talk with me more. Tell me. I know nothing of all you speak about. I know nothing except this little land of mine, and here it seems, it seems—nothing touches us. All the things you speak of—I know nothing of them. They sink in my heart, where I feel a great hollowness. How could I learn about it all? What you speak of—grief—what is that? And that one must know it if one would also rejoice, and what is it to rejoice? I know nothing. And this land of mine that you found so—what was it you called it—lackluster, lifeless—what is it that makes it so? What must I do for my land? Can you tell me?"

The forester then sat down with a troubled face. He laced his fingers together and frowned at them, pondering, and then shook his head.

"I am a poor simple man, sire, hardly a man even, but almost yet a boy. I would not pretend to give counsel to a king! Yet I will tell you what I feel." He looked up eagerly. "This land seems like one under a spell, not an evil enchantment, where dark things happen, but somehow as if there were a line on either side beyond which one could not go, either for joy or sorrow, beauty or ugliness, good or evil, but was always between, in the middle, neither hot nor cold. I would not know how to break that spell. It is not for me to do, nor for one man to do. Perhaps it waits for God to do. Or God waits the hour to do it!"

When the king still sat silent, the forester spoke again. "At least you could see for yourself some of the things of which I have told. You could make a journey. That at least you can do. You could at least come back with a pack of stories to tell your people, who seem about as quiet a lot as any I've ever met up with!"

The king sighed. "Where should I go? Where should I start out?"

The forester laughed. "That is easy!" he said. Since this is the land in the middle, the highway North and South, or the highway East and West will at least take you somewhere else."

The king rose then, and the lad stood up, searching his face. The king drew his hand across his forehead. Then he straightened and smiled at the boy in green. It was a warm smile, though the face was tired, and if his own people had seen him then they would scarce have known him.

"It was good you came, my lad. If you return this way, come again to my castle, and perchance you will find a bit of difference. Now when you go down, would you ask the steward to come to me? I will prepare for this journey. And if there is aught you need, take it. And I wish you well."

He laid his hand on the boy's shoulder. Then he turned to the window, and when the steward came he found his king standing, arms laid across the sill, gazing over the fields to the far mountains. The steward did not know it yet, and the king only dimly sensed it, but the old time had ended.

II

The king traveled as a stonemason, the craft in which he had been trained as a boy. He set out a week after the young forester had gone. First he put the affairs of the kingdom in order—what little needed to be done in that orderly realm—and he tried to explain to the queen. If she had ever known that there was such a thing as madness, she would have called him mad. It was her turn to know astonishment, and of a deeper kind than that of having one's coffee boiling for the first time in one's experience. Finally she looked at him for a long time, and something strange hurt in her chest. At last she put her hand on his and said in a puzzled way, "But I cannot think how each day will be if you are not here." And a little prickle came behind her eyes. "Nor do I understand all that you tell me. But I will try, and I will wait for your return."

Then she stood on the ramparts and watched him go. He traveled west, first riding with a wagoner taking pens of ducks to a farm on the outlying districts of the realm, a pleasant ride through sunny days and cool evenings—not much talk except the prattle of the ducks and now and then a comment from the wagoner, who did not know his passenger. They put up at quiet inns, and at the dawn of the third day they were at the border. The king, all unknown, left the road and disappeared through the hedge, not to be seen again for many weeks by his own subjects.

The mountains there were very steep and sudden, with thick evergreen forests on their slopes. He wondered at himself that he had never wondered before what lay beyond them. It was a stiff climb, and he, while strong, was unused to such, and when he camped for the night his bones ached so he could hardly sleep. He finally stirred himself before dawn, ate a frugal breakfast, not knowing how long it would be before he could replenish his pack, and then climbed on. At daybreak he neared the top, and reached a great rock grey with age and flecked here and there with bearded lichen and little ferns clutching the cracks. Here he stopped and looked back across the valley of his land, just as the sun rose. The sky was all afire, the deep blue of night driven back to green, to gold, to pale yellow, and to rose, and the stars went out as he watched, and all about him birds sang, pealing melodies clear and sweet. Below, the valley lay in soft mist with the river winding dark and small and the road a tiny white track. His heart swelled with the beauty of the world. At last he spoke aloud.

"Farewell, my little land. I wish that you could see the beauty of this dawning or that I might find words to tell you of it. Perhaps even there the day will come when the sun will rise with such...with such..." and then words failed him, and he could only stand silent with tears on his cheeks, before going on.

On the other side the shadows fell long, and the new valley that lay before him seemed dark. Such fields as he could see were brown, and the only road a small track by a wide, shallow river, thick with tumbled stones. Far off he could see great smokes rising, and a haze drifting. He could make out, he thought, in the nearer distance, a cluster of houses close to the river, so he went down, through thorns and clinging cat brier, over loose stone, down where it seemed no man had ever been, down to the edges of the nearest fields. And then he could see they had been parched dry. Surely this had been an early bean field, for the withered, half-grown pods lay there, among the crumbled vines. He had never seen a field like this, but it looked like a plant he had once found in a corner of the potting shed that had been forgotten, all dry and withered so the leaves fell to dust.

"Surely," he said, "it must be there has been no rain. But then how do men live, if the land fails?" And he stood in thought and searched the sky for clouds— but all was clear, except for the haze; the sun, now climbing the sky, smote the earth with heat. He found the road and went on, his feet raising dust at each step. The hedges were withering, now and then a pale flower tried to bloom. And over all there was the taint of smoke—not the cheerful hearth smell of chimney smoke, nor the ingathering smell of autumn leaf piles burning, but the smoke of something lost and dead.

He came at last to the village. A pale, thin child with a smudged face stood by the nearest house and watched him come, then ran inside. A man came out, club in hand, as he drew near.

"What want you?" he growled.

"I am a traveling stonemason," said the king.

"There is no work here. Where did you come from?"

"Yonder, over the mountains, in the land on the other side."

The man stared in amazement.

"Do you have rain there this year?"

74

"What we need, no more, no less. But here..." the king gestured with his hand.

The man came closer. The king could see more clearly now his lined face, his gaunt black eyes.

"Is there food there for all?"

"Yes, all we need."

"Have they not come to seize it?"

"They? Who are they?"

"The enemy, the destroyers, the cursed ones who take what little a man has and burn what shelter he has left."

"We know none such as that. I did not know such men lived."

The man pointed to the distance where the sky was dark with smoke. "Go there, and see for yourself," he said in a trembling voice.

And the king went.

It was a week or more later that the king lay, wounded, in the hut of a peasant on the edge of the town. The face of the woman bending over him, when he opened his eyes at last, seemed to his befuddled mind like the queen's, only more gentle and more tired. Outside there was the soft sound of rain.

The woman bathed his shoulder, and it stung fearfully, the pain going deep down his arm. She smiled at him.

"It heals well. If we had more food to give, you would be stronger again fast. But now the rains have returned, and we can feel the earth coming alive again under our feet." She bathed his face and smoothed his pillow. "And now the war is done and the enemy withdrawn, with a new pact between us. Surely God has been good to us in spite of all the death we have wrought upon ourselves."

The king lay wordless, looking up at her. He began to remember all he had seen—the field of dead, the weeping women, the charred and shattered houses, the hate in the eyes of the men who had attacked him as he walked, all unknowing, into the middle of a foray. Most of all he remembered the wan and frightened children, and he thought of the calm, rosy faces of his own. He was too weak to speak; he closed his eyes, and all the sights that he had seen flashed before him again, a raving, noisy, terrifying train. Then he saw again the last sunrise over his own land, the golden splendor filling all the sky, the quiet land lying simple and at peace. He opened his eyes. Beside the woman now stood a man, dark and troubled, looking down at him. The man pulled up a stool and sat close to him.

His eyes were kind, but weary and sunken. His hands trembled a bit, so he clasped them together.

"Friend," he said. "You came unknown amongst us in a dark and fearful hour. Now the wind changes and a new time comes, perhaps, for this seared and sorrowing land. Now you lie here mending, and we will do what we can to strengthen you—though we have lost nearly all. But there is still time for a late harvest— now the gentle rains come. When you are well enough you will go on. Already many take the road, to find sufficient food until our own fields yield again, or to seek new homes. Those of us who stay will have much work." He looked at his hands that still trembled. "Nor have we much strength left to labor. But you..." and he looked long into the king's face... "where did you journey from, and for what?"

But the woman set a steaming cup into the man's

hands and said, chiding, "Give him a sup first, he is too weak to speak much now." So the man raised the king's head and he sipped the brew, and felt it flow all through him. It was hot and strong, seeming to reach down to his toes and to the tips of his ears, and suddenly into his mind came the remembrance of the young forester, and the boiling coffee. He looked up into the man's face and smiled, saying, "It is hot, it is good. It gives a man courage."

The man laid him back on the pillow and said, "Now tell us who you are."

"I come from the land on the other side of the mountains. There I have lived all my life. It is a peaceful little land, where all labor and have enough." He stopped, not knowing how to continue, how much to tell, how to find words for it. The woman set her hand on her man's shoulder, and they both looked at him, patient and a bit puzzled.

"But I came to know, one day, that the world must be very different, that we lived only in a kind of dead center, that there was such a thing as grief, and such a thing as joy, and such a thing as great beauty, and great evil, but I knew it not, nor did my people. Nor did I know that there was need in the world, that any others lived except as we lived. So I decided to journey, to see for myself, and to return to my people to tell them if I could. At least to have a tale that would set

their minds awondering. Now, what I have seen...
I can scarcely grasp. And if I, who have seen, can
scarcely begin to fathom it, how can I hope to tell
my people, to speak of it to them...?" He stopped,
exhausted. The two still looked at him.

"You speak of your people. What were you to them?"

"I was their king," the king said simply. "Now I
must seek the way to reach the hearts of my people, to
open their eyes, to show them at least how little we
know, how little we feel, how much we must do, and
at length how powerless we are—as I lie here."

The three were silent in the little hut. Outside the
soft sound of rain continued, and a cuckoo called
insistently and near at hand.

"Tell me," said the king. "What will touch the small
hearts of my people? What will break the spell that
binds them?"

"Sire," said the man, "no man can tell you that.
Perhaps it will come to you, as you mend, to find the
right way."

"I wish to mend quickly now, and return. We must
give help to this troubled land. We must share with
you," and the king moved to sit up.

"Wait," said the man. "Perhaps God has brought
you low to give your own heart time to understand all
that has come to you. Rest now, and take a little time
of peace. I am not one to give counsel to a king, yet I

know how little man can do, unless God sets the seal."

"I praise Him," said the king, "that I fell into your hands."

"Nay, we praise Him that you have come."

So the king stayed and grew stronger bit by bit. On the third day he went out and sat on a bench by the wall and looked at the havoc all around. He watched on the road as the wagons passed, some going south to seek a new home, some carrying the dead for burial, some bringing new-hewn logs for building, some bringing in from outlying farms the ill, the homeless, or the old. Each day he watched, and his heart bore more and more. And on the sixth day he was strong enough to climb into a wagon and go out with the man to a distant farm from which there had been no word.

"He is the beekeeper, and his wife, and one small child. A great strong man, hardy and brave—but they have suffered much in the drought. And the enemy came that way first. I fear for them."

And they rode on in silence. By noon they came within sight of the cottage, the beehouse, the neat hives. But all was silent. There was no sign of fire, but the yard was trampled and the gate thrown down. When the man called, the silence only deepened and grew thick. They climbed down over the wagon wheel, pushed through the tumbled yard, and went up to the open door. There they stopped, and their indrawn breath was the only sound. Here death had indeed visited. But as they stared in horror and in grief, they saw the child still lived; he raised a terror-numbed, ashy little face and whimpered. The king gazed long at him, the great black eyes that seemed to look at nothing but fear, the little hands like claws, the sunken temples; then he knelt and gathered him up against his shoulder, and turned with a tear-streaked face to the man.

"Is this not the answer? Will this not melt a heart of stone? Is any heart so small this child cannot find room there?"

And so it was to be.

The next day the king set out for home. He went south on the road to the highway, knowing he could not cross the mountain with his burden and the weakness from his wounds. In two days he reached the highway and turned east. Along the road there had been so many fleeing from the ravage of the war that few had cast more than one pitying glance at the child resting against his shoulder. But on the highway there were many prosperous and well-clad, who looked in distaste and dismay at the king and his burden. So he covered the child with a tattered shawl, and sought— also out of his own poverty—the poorest inns, and gave the child all that he could beg or purchase—though the little one would scarcely eat. On the fifth day he came unrecognized into the borders of his own land. At the first farm he stopped. The good wife stood in the door and stared at him. There was something in his face she dimly knew, yet how could she know anyone so soiled and torn and tired, so gaunt of face and sad? She called her man, and he stood at her elbow, for a moment dumbstruck, before he stepped forward suddenly.

"Sire!" he cried. "Dear master, what has befallen you?"

Then the king smiled, and a great relief flooded his heart.

"I am coming home after a long journey. Now I would ask two things of you. First, start the word throughout the realm that the king would speak to the people before this night falls, by the castle ramparts, so all who can will gather. Then I would beg your wagon for the rest of this journey, for my burden, though light, is more than my strength can carry."

Then the man called his sons and sent them out with the word, and he fetched his wagon, and the king climbed in while the man leapt into the seat and took the reins himself. But the good wife ran out with a bowl of milk, and would not let them go until she had placed it in the king's hands and seen him drink. He handed it back empty and said, "That was a blessed draught, for which I give you thanks." Then he gathered his burden more closely to him, and the wagon started on.

In the long late spring twilight they drew near the castle. Behind them on the road there were many people, and wagons, and down the lanes more gathering. But there was little noise and no confusion, and in all a wonder grew and grew. On the ramparts the queen waited. She ran down as the first wagon came. With haste and a beating heart she ran up to it, and looked in the king's face, laying a hand on his knee. He looked down at her.

"Do not be afraid, though all things now change for us."

Then he stood up, holding his burden against his shoulder, and gazed out over the people that gathered closer, wondering and still.

At last he spoke, his voice clear and strong.

"Dear people, dwellers in this sheltered little land. Many days ago I set forth, clear to the borders and straight over the mountain into the unknown beyond. This I did, as your king, because of a simple traveler who all unknowing spoke words that shook my heart. He spoke of weather I had never known, of needs I had never seen, of death coming to the young and fair, of flowering trees, of great joy that filled the heart. All this was so strange to me the words were like another language. What lay beyond this quiet little land? What lay over us like a smothering mist to keep our hearts unquestioning, unquesting, our days so small and mild? So I set out. And I went indeed into need, into a dark land where men struggled for the light, and where the hand of love reached out to me also." And in slow

words, plain and bare, he told them of the drought, the hate, the war; destruction, death, and pain. He told them of his wound, and of the peasant who had succored him. And how he searched for a way to tell them, his people, to clear their eyes, to help them find with him the way for them now.

"And then, in the last farm, I found this child, orphaned, starving, stiff with fear. He has come to us, the first from beyond our borders that have stood too long."

Then he drew back the tattered shawl. The child lay with his cheek against the king's shoulder, the thin little hands clasped about his neck. The king turned slowly and the child raised his head and looked out over all the people to the setting sun. And in the west the rosy light grew until the air glowed and they seemed to be standing in the midst of the light. But the people looked only at the child, no movement except that here and there a mother put her arms around her own young and drew them suddenly close; and hands were pressed to hearts that suddenly pained. And a sound grew, very soft and low, that had not been heard before in all that land—the sound of many people weeping.

So it was that a new time came. For as there was the sound of weeping then, so also there came the sound of singing—not a tuneless humming but songs of praise, songs of joy, songs of courage. They seemed to spring up out of the earth. And men labored long, and great wains rolled out with food for the hungry. Looms hummed late in the night by lamplight, and the wagons carried coverlets and clothes. The sick came to be healed, and some to die. Homeless children found father and mother again. And North, South, East, and West the king sent travelers to come back with knowledge of the world—and the map makers tore up the old maps and started out afresh.

The people dared much, and some suffered for it. They knew what it was to be tired to the bone, sick, beaten, yet not for anything would they go back to the old way. Winters grew longer, cold, and the snows more wild—but spring also became a time of bursting blossom, of burgeoning earth; summers were hot but the cool of evening more blessed, and the harvests so heavy there were hardly hands enough to gather them in, while the trees flamed on every side.

And the children grew more naughty but also more warm of heart and full of joy. While a father now and then had to lay a hand to his son he also could look more deeply into his eyes, and trust grew.

And it was a time when grief came, more than a word, an actual thing. But also then joy came. And the greatest pain was the cold heart, the offered help that was spurned, the hand held out that met no answering clasp; that, and the sense that neither they for all their labors, nor any man, could heal all the hurts of the world, until the new time came for every heart.

And some may ask, what became of the child? In a certain way it would make a happier story to be able to write that the child thrived and grew bonny and strong and lived long. But such was not to be. Perhaps by all the hunger and need some deep hurt had been done to his little body that no broth and coddled eggs and loving words could mend. The little one died after many days, but first his small face had come to smile, and the great eyes to grow alight, and he laughed and sang even as he faded away. Then the women wept and the men stood with grief-stricken faces, helpless, and the children stood beside the little bier with flowers in their hands and tears on their cheeks, and understood best of all, perhaps, that God had sent the child for a purpose, and for His own purpose had called him home.

They laid him in a little grave set round by birches, at the roadside, and on the stone the king himself graved the words:

> *In memory of the child, who led us*
> *from the land that was neither hot*
> *nor cold, into God's wind and weather.*

promise

I who have sinned against God
stand cold and empty-handed,
desert under my feet
with no hope of flowering,
athirst where there is no spring,
in a land where no manna falls
and no voice speaks—

Ah, but somewhere
my brother loves me,
from far, from unknown places
my brother speaks for me,
my brother calls me,
my brother longs with a pure love
to break the spell of the barren land,
to rend the dry earth that binds me—

Then from the vast, brassy, barren sky
comes the small cloud,
the gathering sweet rain!
Then comes the warm wind
and the sound of bells,
the sound of running feet
and glad voices calling;
the flowers spring up and the birds
beat with glad wings about my shoulders.

And a Child takes my hand, crying
"Come—the Kingdom awaits!"

THE SECRET FLOWER

NOTE

This story takes place in the England of the Middle Ages, specifically during the months from June 1382 to February 1383. The year 1381 had seen the upheaval and apparent fruitlessness of the Peasants' Revolt, and the beginning of the Lollard Movement that was to be strong for the next fifty years or more, with far-reaching influence. Wyclif had already faced persecution and retired to Lutterworth, and his "Poor Priests" with their English Bibles were slowly beginning to be seen about the countryside and in the towns. The terrible years of the Black Death (1348–49) were close enough to be a horror still, and the plague had visited enough since then to be an ever-threatening reality. The established church was corrupt, sterile, hypocritical, and wealthy, while the commons were poor, and misery of every sort walked abroad. Still, the hearts of many were full of courage and a simple faith, and certainly the vision then of brotherhood and Christ's Truth catches our eye even through the intervening centuries.

The city which Simon finally glimpses was no real city in the historical sense, but surely in those times of suffering and seeking it was there, as it always exists somewhere; it is built upon faith and by the living Spirit directing the hands and minds of mortal men, and it continues only by grace and by a daily fight against evil and for the purity which alone is God's. It is an eternal City and hearts in every age are stirred with longing for it, and hear the call to dwell within it; yet many, like Simon, find it only at the end or not at all. It is with a living sense of kinship with those seekers of the past and of the future that this story has been undertaken.

"...That is just the strength in our innermost being,

that after all, in the last depths of our hearts
this faith (in a redemption of love)
slumbers and cannot be killed.

Yes, in each of us wells up
that source of faith in life
    and hope of love
which overcomes everything evil and negative.

    We could no longer live at all
    if we no longer had this faith.
      It may be buried,
                  withered,
                          or distorted,
    but it is there.
    For there is living in all of us,
      HOPE in the future,
        WILL to community,
           JOY in the unity of life.

The spirit of LOVE is hidden in every man
    and in the whole creation.
At certain moments of exaltation it comes over us
with such a force and power
    that we are overcome and cast to the ground,
    so that all scruples vanish like soap bubbles
    and we feel: Yes, that is reality,
    this love, this faith in the unity of humanity;
    the certainty that everything living
    belongs together really is the truth.
Pilate asks: 'What is truth?'
Jesus answers him: 'I am the Truth.'
    Do we not all feel, in these decisive hours
      when we are really honest
      and stand face to face with eternal truth,
    that He really is?"

                 Eberhard Arnold, in "Love Redeemed"

The Secret Flower

This child was born to men of God:
Love to the world was given;
 In him were truth and beauty met,
 On him was set
At birth, the seal of heaven.

He came the Word to manifest,
Earth to the stars he raises;
 The teacher's errors are not his,
 The Truth he is:
No man can speak his praises.

He evil fought and overcame,
He took from death the power;
 To all that follow where he goes
 At last he shows
The Kingdom's secret Flower.

The secret Flower shall bloom on earth
In them that have beholden;
 The heavenly Spirit shall be plain
 In them again,
As first it was of olden.

The Spirit like a light shall shine,
Evil himself dispelling.
    The Spirit like a wind shall blow,
    And Death shall go
Unfeared in her own dwelling.

And by the Spirit shall be known
The bearers of the Flower;
    Yea, they shall stand in all men's sight
    Amid the light
God sent to be their power.

German, 17th Century
Paraphrased by
  Eleanor Farjeon

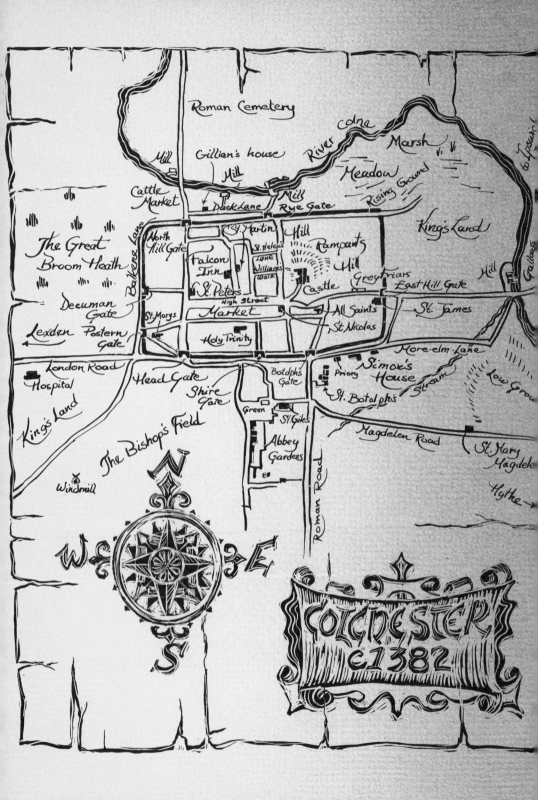

the secret flower

Colchester was an ancient town full of memories. The Celts had first settled there. Buried under its 14th Century cobbles were the coins and pagan graves of Rome; the Norman keep had been built partly of Roman stone, and the streets followed the old pattern. Its heroine was Queen Boadicea. Its spirit was independent; it bred rebels like Wat Tyler and John Ball, and was to become a stronghold of Lollardism in the 1400's. It lay close enough to the coast to have a sense of blue distance and far places; from time to time strange mariners appeared in its markets, come up from the Hythe to see a foreign town; and the gulls followed the River Colne up from the sea to wheel and cry over the marshy meadows by the Middle Mill and the King's Lands, reminding the land-bound citizens that not so far away was the end of the world they knew and the beginning of the unknown.

It was a sturdy town, and lively, allotted five yearly fairs, ten parishes with a cheerful mingling of bells, the Abbey of St. John prosperous and handsome just outside the walls, and a leper hospital at a healthy distance. Lord Fitz-Walter rode in from Lexden now and then and made a stir in the streets. If one went in and out at Head Gate on the south side of the wall one could see the windmill wheeling down on the Bishop's Fields. The river was a constant element; the three watermills clacked away from dawn till late afternoon, and the tanners and fullers toiled on its banks, while the wind often blew laden with the smell of old fish and drying nets. Many a tidy garden had its paths paved with the bleached white of oystershells, some from the ancient heaps left by the Romans.

There were such shells on the paths in Simon Beston's garden, crushed and broken almost to a powder now, but he had never wondered whose ingenious rake had dragged them up from the river bottom, or whose hands had prized them open, with a tool long since lost. Other men's labors he gave little heed to, especially that centuries old, for he was deeply wrapt by his own, care-ridden and joyless, prosperous and proud, lonely as the heron that stood long hours in the marshes below the

Lower Mill but unlike the heron, with no young to whom to carry home the trophy. He was obscure and nameless yet was one of a new man in England, enterprising and independent, shrewd and industrious, with a quiet, steady eye to his own outward welfare. What happened inwardly . . . Mass and the confession and communion at Easter took care of that, he told himself. Though now and then, especially with the dawn when something woke him, doubt like a great grey abyss loomed under him, he swung out over it helpless in terror, and sweating, scrambled out of his massive bed to cling to the window sill gazing over the garden and pasture land to St. Botolph's and beyond it mistily rising the towers of St. John's Abbey. Such times were few, but they left him shaken and questioning for a day or two till the accustomed rounds and the press of business swept over him and carried him on uncaring.

But that doubt was a hidden jewel set deep in his mind, and now and then it caught the light to burn forth clear and undeniable. Perhaps that was why the heart had leapt when he had heard John Ball preach some ten years ago now, on pride and lechery and covetousness and sloth, thundering out against the Church itself and calling all humble and true men to link hands as brothers and rise together; but John Ball went on his way and the jeweled fire died amid Simon's own sorrows. Now and then he heard the name of the priest, with a little flicker deep inside, and then in the mutinous, terrible times of the uprising—Simon had drawn the shutters close, stopped his ears, covered his eyes, and spoken to no one.

As for Wat Tyler, he was a loud and insolent fellow, who had lived in a daub and wattle hut, now pulled down and turned to dust, on St. Helen's Lane, in the town itself; he had served in the French War and had killed his erstwhile master during the London insurrection, Simon had heard, which hadn't surprised him, and now was himself dead and his ready tongue silenced forever; many a time Simon had heard him pounding on the table in The Falcon and sounding forth for the power of the Commons and the smashing of all wealth. But no fire gleamed in Simon in response. Why? He never wondered. Perhaps the lovelessness and arrogance of the man left him without warmth. Perhaps also he feared a bit for his own house, so snug and fine, and for his well-swept, well-stocked shop.

That piece of land outside the town had been his from his father's time. He had been a young man when he set his eyes on it for a house for several reasons. First, he wanted a house, a good, sturdy one, and one to be proud of, no patched and mended stuck-together-anyhow shelter, but a house made to last, with his initials carved over the door and the mercer's sign hung out. Also he had his eye on the spot as a likely one for business—outside the walls it is true, but near the juncture of the London Road and the old Roman Road by Botolph's Gate, and it was a busy thoroughfare with much traffic coming up from Magdalen Road also, or the comings to and fro from the big Abbey. Many had scoffed at the time, but had shaken their heads later at his shrewdness and all around the town now outside of the walls business had spread; he had quite started a trend, which helped him, too. Also ever since all of the town in the North Hill Gate section had gone up in flames when he was a boy, he had feared city fires, and he wanted a place at a safe distance, not crowded shoulder to shoulder with its fellows and vulnerable to their careless sparks. And, perhaps, though he never knew how big a part this played, he wanted a fair, new place for Hawise. But she didn't live longer than there was time to plot out the garden and set out the apple trees with him, and she only saw them bloom once.

The house had been for him, when he built it, pretentious, but not so now that he was well-to-do; now it was suitable. It stood directly on More-elm Lane, on either side it a brick wall with neat, solid gates, surrounding the garden. To the right as one went in was the hall, beyond the screens, and to the left a door to the shop, whose wide shutter opened on the street. Directly ahead one glimpsed the kitchen, and beyond, the buttery. Above the shop and kitchen was a second story with storeroom in front, and chamber behind, both reached by a winding stair from the kitchen. The hall itself had a fireplace built in the far wall, quite a new-fangled thing, and also the kitchen had its built-in hearth, and above it Simon's chamber had its fire-place, so the house was serviceable and fine. No man could ask more for comfort within. And without? Well, he took pride in husbandry, for all he was a mercer by trade. Beyond the buttery he had added a shed and cowstall; against the east garden wall were set the hives, among the apple trees, and beyond them the chicken roost and the vegetable garden with well-kept rows of cabbages, leeks, lettuce, kale, and beans. There was a duck pond with a big willow overhanging it, and beyond it the land dropped off to pastures, a wandering small stream, marshland, and in the far distance southeasterly the parish of St. Mary Magdalen's, and past it the river; northeasterly was the cluster of abbey buildings with his own parish of St. Botolph's huddling nearer at hand.

The garden Hawise had planned was in the angle of the house, near the wall; it was fragrant with rose-mary and saffron, thyme and lavender; corn poppies grew there, and white violets in the spring; roses, blue scabious, and herb Robert. Simon tended them all, partly out of love for growing things, partly out of pride, and partly out of a lonely, sorrowing memory for someone that, as far as he could remember, he had once loved.

II

Simon, on that fresh, sparkling June morning, knelt in the storeroom before the large oaken chest where he kept his stock of gloves. He picked them over carefully, laying some aside in small piles on the floor to be taken below to the shop. When he finished he let the lid fall to with a thump, and then turned to a coffer that had a peacock painted on the lid, a gay strutting bird with a spread tail and bright eye; with the back of his sleeve he smoothed and dusted it, for it had belonged to Hawise, and he remembered her delight in it. Now it held the richest belts and he opened it to finger them over and take out three or four; he chose only one that was jeweled, as they were too precious to display much for fear of theft, and not greatly in demand in the town of Colchester—nevertheless, one girdle gleaming with pearl and emerald would signify that there was more wealth, perhaps, hidden away for one who could afford it. He chose also a wide red belt embossed with dragons and a knight at arms, with a golden clasp, and two more modest, green-braided ones.

When he had gathered them together with the gloves he went into his chamber to go below, and then stopped to listen to the voices he had heard dimly in the back of his mind while he had been working. One was Margrit, the old woman who kept his house, and the other was a man's voice, and unknown. He was puzzled that anyone had come, for Ben, the great mastiff chained by the kitchen door, always raised a fury when a stranger appeared. With his foot on the top stair, Simon paused. He could see only a patch of sun on the well-scrubbed floor, and as he listened, he heard the bell ringing for Terce across the fields from the Abbey. Simon waited for the strange voice to speak again, but it was Margrit.

"You'd best eat a bit before you go on. The master wouldna' mind. He's not stingy for all he's not generous."

"Have you no mistress, then?" The man's voice was clear and fresh, with a gentleness in it. Simon could not place it, nor its inflection; certainly not an Essex man, anyway, nor one out of the North.

"No, nor little ones here, either. Mistress died of the plague, ten years ago now, and a baby daughter too, and another on the way. It was a sad time, and the town bad hit, also, though not as bad as that first spell of it, when I was a girl. That was bad beyond all thinking—half the town lying dead and mostly unburied, and the priests either dead or fled away from fear, but that was over thirty years ago now and one forgets a bit except sometimes in the night or when the sickness strikes again as it did when Mistress Hawise died."

Simon stood and waited. He could not go down now. The old time flooded over him again, the terror and the stunned sorrow, Hawise lying cold and still and the child crying in fever; how no one would come to help but old Margrit, not so old then, and her idiot son Piers, and how together they had made the bier and he had fetched the priest who all hasty and fearful had mumbled the service, and the lonely walk down the lane in the drizzling morning to the burying with no bearers but the bier laid on the haywain and the old horse plodding; and the fresh earth being thrown in the grave with a sickening sound; and the next day it all to do over again with the little lass. And then the days afterwards empty and cold, no one coming near but old Margrit from her hovel down the lane, the shop closed, the street quiet, until after the early frosts when the contagion passed, and fear began to dwindle; people spoke again, and St. Denis Fair opened as usual in a brilliant October with the townsmen gay and noisy, here and there one in mourning, but all eager to put death behind them and make the most of the day.

"It is a brave house for one man alone," said the stranger.

"That's how he chose it; that's how it is to be," said Margrit flatly. There was a little silence.

"Where be you from, mister?" There was a respectful curiosity in Margrit's voice that puzzled Simon. He heard her begin to shell peas, the pods snapping open and the peas rattling into the bowl.

"Here, I can as well do that, while you do something I cannot do," said the stranger's voice, and there was a little stir while the job was handed over, and Margrit stumped over to the table. The patch of sunlight was blotted out. Simon could hear dough being plumped and rolled for a pasty.

"Where be you from, and what is your trade, mister, if I may ask?" she repeated.

"I come from a city a ways from here, and I am a shepherd," said the man quietly.

"Have you been here for St. John's Fair?"

"Well, in a way, perhaps." The man chuckled a little. "Though I brought no sheep to sell, and mayhap bought none either."

Margrit thumped the dough. "Your master will chide you."

"No, not mine. Maybe you rightfully do not know my master. He bids me travel about now and then, to seek the sheep that have lost their true shepherd, or never found him."

"You speak in riddles, mister. Where is it you come from, and what nonsense is this you speak? It smacks a bit of the time so lately passed, just a year ago, and some of the words we heard then. That is over and done with now, and best forgotten."

The man went on shelling peas, and Simon, as if he had been drawn by a magnet, came slowly down the stairs. At his step, the man looked up and smiled, and Margrit bobbed a curtsy. Simon stood there at the bottom, his hands full of belts and gloves, and stared at the man. He was bearded and brown-visaged, with piercing blue eyes and dark lashes like star points; he wore a dusty grey tunic and hood, and broidered over his heart a bright blue flower. He laid the bowl aside and stood up, looking Simon through and through. The sunlit silence lengthened.

Finally, "Sit," said Simon, motioning to the bench, and the man sat again, taking up the pea-shelling, which was nearly done.

"You've come a long way?" asked Simon, though he knew not why.

"That depends," said the man. "From where you are, mayhap quite a way," and he flashed Simon a smile, "but not too far to be reached."

"Who is your master?"

"None better," came the quiet answer. Margrit waited for Simon to flare up in impatience.

"Has he no name?"

"If I told you, would you believe me?" The man let his hands rest and looked at Simon squarely. "There are things a man will not believe, even when he hears them with his own ears. What if I told you that my master was Our Lord himself?"

"The man is mad," muttered Simon, and turned to go. But he checked himself and turned back for another question.

"What manner of city is it, then, where you dwell with such a master?"

The man bent his head a bit, as if to gauge his words, then his voice came soft and joyful.

"A city of music, and little children; a city where peace dwells, and no sorrow but what it is shared and turned to blessing; a city of labor but no strife, where no man speaks but in honesty and love; where sin is turned back at the gate and driven out not by the sword of hate but by a seal of purity; a city beyond our words to reckon. . . ." His voice died off, and then he looked up, such a light in his face as Simon had never seen. "I wish I could show it to you, brother." His voice had a longing in it.

Simon stood motionless and stunned.

"And where is this place?" he finally dragged out.

"North, and then west. Over the hills. A long way, and a hard way, full of danger. But not too far for every man. A fair blue flower grows there that grows in no other land," and his hand went to his heart.

"Do you take me for a fool, to believe all this?"

"It isn't for me to say," came the voice of the man, and he smiled at Simon, "but if you do, then you are God's fool, at least."

The shop bell tinkled insistently. Simon's hands on

the belts and gloves were sweating. He turned away and went into the shop, letting the heavy door swing to behind him. The kitchen was silent for a while, Margrit too dumbstruck to finish her pasty and the man sitting there peacefully with his hands on his knees, the bowl of the shelled peas on the floor between his feet.

"A daft way you have of speaking," she said at last, and slung the round of dough into a deep pan, trimming the edges with deft movements. "Methinks he was angry."

The man sighed and stood up. "I have cheese and bread in my wallet," he said, slapping it, "and a ways to go today, so I'll be moving. Say farewell to your master, and mayhap someday I'll set eyes on his face again."

He stepped out into the sun, under the blossoming apple trees that hummed and quivered with bees, and his eyes rested on the yellow hives, and the trim wall, and then on the big dog that lay at his feet with head between his paws, his eyes turned up, and his tail flapping.

"Good fellow," said the man, stopping to pat him. Then he swung off down the path, out the gate, and left along the London Road. The gate swung to with a little click behind him. Far off the Abbey bell rang Sext, and all the other bells chimed in, mellow and soft in the noon sun.

III

With the coming of evening Simon went out of the house door to lower the lattice and shutter over the shop front; a fastening had caught in a rose vine and he pricked his finger freeing it, and was sucking at the blood when Derek Munsley came by with a string of fish from the river. He lingered a moment. Simon turned back to his work, but Derek had too much talk in his head to be daunted.

"Do you remember the day a year ago, happen, Simon?"

"Best forget these days now. Over and done," muttered Simon, as he slammed to the shutter and bent back the rose vine.

"Wat Tyler's forgotten them, dead and buried no one knows where, all his brash talk and free notions gone to earth. And John Ball too, with his fancy rhymes and fetching phrases. What good did it do us, or anyone! The world's the same, and always will be."

Simon stopped at his doorstep and looked back at Derek.

"If ye think that," he said, "why breathe!" Then he went inside, to the dim quiet and the emptiness, shutting the door on the road and Derek standing there with a blank face, and in his head his own words echoing, "If ye think that, why breathe!" Had he rightly said it to Derek, or to himself?

Why indeed breathe; why get up in the morning and wrangle in the market and count the silver and wait for the folk to come into the shop to buy; why go to Mass and hear the priest Fulcun muttering at the altar, and trouble at that picture of Doomsday over the door, with the flames of Hell and the devils torturing the damned; why go to The Falcon for a draft of ale in the quiver of a hope to find a friendly face and an honest word; why go down to the church-yard ever and anon to lay a posy on Hawise's grave and the little one beside it; why prune the apple trees and harvest the honey and breed the cow and gather the eggs and weed the garden and put back the tile on the roof when the tempests displaced it; why keep old Margrit in the kitchen and her lazy lout of a son, Piers. "If the world's the same and always will be," he thought, "time might as well stand still and the sand stop running through the glass. I might as well be done with it now. What little I had of joy is under the ground now and what little I knew of God is false words and a foul priest." He latched the shutter from the inside and began to put the shop to rights, in the dimness of the light that came from the hall door. In the kitchen he could hear Margrit groaning and grunting to herself as she fixed his supper, beans and bacon by the smell of it.

Then he pulled out into the open what he had pushed under all day, the gnawing, haunting memory. That man, that strange man this morning. The look in his eye, the warm fresh look, the smile at the corner of his eye, the clear undertone to his voice, the bright blue flower sewn on the breast of his worn tunic, the look of his hands as he slid the peas from their shells, the clear glance that could not be withstood. And those riddling words that rang with truth.

All day long like a bright spark dancing among the dark memories of a year ago the image of this man had come; now the spark ignited the dry dust of the past and all flared up newly revealed. Somewhere a man walked who was free within and without; in whose eyes there seemed to be no shadow of fear, who seemed to have not mirth nor bawdiness nor loud foolery but a true joy. And the fair city he spoke of, it must be Heaven itself!

Simon left the dusky shop and stepped over into the empty reach of the hall; with his arms folded over his breast he paced back and forth from the hearth to the screens, and let the full flood of memory sweep over him. A man could not have gone through that time indifferent, not if he had a beating heart at all. He remembered first the rumors and the wild hopes in the town, set alongside the scoffing and belittling of others. What would ever hope to change the old order, said some? Wealth was wealth, and power was power; the poor were poor and never would be otherwise except in Paradise. But throughout Essex the word went that the time was come, that the boy King was to be faced and would be found favoring the Commons, that the fat friars and proud abbots were to be thrown down, and all men joined equally under their true Head, as it would have it in Scripture (if only all men could read it for themselves, not hear it mumbled in an ancient tongue). But the burgesses wagged their heads and counseled caution and warned against treason. Simon had listened and kept his own opinion to himself, if indeed he knew it; he remembered John Ball and felt a flicker of hope; he remembered Wat Tyler and felt a wave of disgust.

But then, like thunderheads piling up in the west, the storm gathered, silent at first, but dark and overhanging. Essex was rising, went the word! A few men vanished from town and their wives went about with dull faces. Mid-June came, and each day dawned taut and expectant, and at last the riders came in from London one hot, dusty noon. The King, young Richard, had granted all! He had pledged himself to the Commons! Justice was done at last! And Simon listened bleakly, feeling the world turned topsy-turvy.

After that the thunder broke, and like gall the once sweet words burned on the tongues of those who had brought the news. London was in murder and riot; the King had betrayed his pledge; Wat Tyler was dead, and John Ball seized for a heretic and traitor; the King's men were marching against the Commons at Billericay.

And then followed the darkest time of all. He remembered standing by Head Gate as the first stragglers of the peasants came into town, sweatstreaked and wild. There had been riots in the market, with the Commons crying for support, and the burgesses shouting them down; the bailiffs were called out, and even as the town authorities strove for order, the Earl of Buckingham's men came marching in, and the last dim hope any man had held that the old power had power no longer, dwindled to a little dust under the trampling feet. In place of the murdered chief justice, Sudbury, Tressilian was carried in on a litter, with a cool level stare, and the Bloody Assize began.

Simon laid his arms on the carved mantel over the hearth, and put his head on them, half sick with the memory. For all he had seen a bit of life and thought he had a strong stomach, the hanging and quartering that had gone on that week had shaken him fearfully; he never went by the junction of St. Martin's Lane and High Street without a shudder, and the cobbles yet looked brown to him, and even a faint stench of blood still. The gallows past East Mill Gate and over the river had been black with vultures for weeks.

And then this man, like an ambassador from a foreign land speaking a foreign tongue. . .a place of no fear, no hating, no sorrow.

He raised his head listening, for he heard Piers outside fetching up water from the well, and mingling with it from the street a singer, with a familiar tune, but English words that fell new on his ears.

> *Thou hast brought forth thy holy son*
> *That man's redemption might be won;*
> *He shall forgive and all men shrive*
> *From evil.*
> *Our present help is come*
> *To bring us joy eternal*
> *And out of exile home.*

Simon heard Piers go lumbering into the house with a full bucket, and he drew his sleeve across his eyes as if to brush the mist from them. He suddenly knew he was weary to the bone, and where his heart had been numb and cold, there was now a great aching.

IV

Next morning, being a Wednesday, was market. Simon woke in a cool dim dawn, feeling somehow that the world was different, but not knowing why. After a bowl of porridge and a beaker of cider, he and Piers started out, Piers pushing a barrow with their gear in it, through Botolph's Gate, already thronging with farmers and tradesmen going the same way. They went straight, then left past All Saints, into the market. In the bustle and stir there, the voices sounded loud and raw, or tired to desperation. The banter and merriment seemed thin; beneath it lay a bleakness that smote Simon; he looked about and paused, while Piers tugged at the barrow and grunted at him to move on.

Their stall was set up at the eastern end, where one caught cross-traffic as well as those who strolled around fingering goods and taking their time. As the morning broke fresh and fair the crowds came. The faces Simon saw, even the ones not new to him, were strange now, and he was so mazed by studying them that Piers, standing back, nudged him now and then when a likely sale was all but ignored. He had sold the green braided belts he had fetched down the day before from the storeroom, and a small blue purse with a white violet stamped on it, and two needle cases with silver needles in them, when the lady came along, with a Maltese spaniel on her arm, and a waiting woman behind. She was feeding the dog morsels of fine white bread from a wallet at her side. She fingered Simon's stuff idly.

"Have ye not any blue silk? Last time I was by ye

had blue silk, at a fair price. This russet would make me look like a Poor Priest!"

"No blue silk, mistress, but Friday there will be. But here is a blue girdle, straight from London."

The little dog yawned, showing two rows of white, sharp teeth and a long pink tongue; he licked the end of his nose and whined for more bread.

"Friday I may come, or I may not, but have it here all the same," and she idly turned away. A beggar was in her path, an old man with a grey face and shriveled legs, rheumy blue eyes and sunken lips. Speechless he held out his hand to her. She lifted her skirts carefully and stepped around him, her face cold. Simon stood with the blue girdle in his hands and watched; the beggar scuttered off crablike. Simon put his hand to his heart, where the ache was, and Piers nudged him as a fat goodwife stood there with her fingers on a small red wallet.

"You are asleep today, Master Simon. I could have waited here till Doomsday," she joshed. "Come, give me the price of this, and make it fair, and make haste. I want this home before it spoils in the heat," and she motioned to a mesh bag of cod over her arm.

Simon hastened and took her silver, and she went off, her broad skirts swinging. And now the Abbot himself came by, two chaplains at his heels. He stopped long enough to run a stale eye over Simon's goods, and then proceeded on. Simon saw the beggar, who had huddled behind an empty stall, come creeping forth, his hand held out to Father Abbot. With a little gesture, the Abbot indicated his will, and one of the chaplains dug into his purse, and dropped a coin in the beggar's hand. The old man slid away again, this time toward the alley where an alehouse stood. Simon watched him out of sight.

Piers nudged him again. Before him stood a little girl, her face besmudged and her blue smock dusty. Her eyes scarce reached above the rim of the stall, and her fingers clutched the top, their tips pressed white beneath their dirt. She gazed up at him. Simon leaned over toward her.

"What is it, my little lass?"

"My mother went to buy clogs, and I have lost her and myself, too," and she began to weep soundlessly. While Piers stared at him, Simon smiled and came around the stall to her. With the edge of his tunic he wiped her face.

"I'll take thee where clogs are sold and likely she'll be there. We'll find her, never fear, and likely she's looking for thee, too. Watch the goods, Piers." And turning his back on his business, Simon walked off holding the little girl's hand. She took his trustingly, and the feel of her little hard palm in his was very strange. As they went past the flower stalls, Simon could feel her dragging, so he stopped and let her look them over. She seemed less frightened now, and he,

not knowing how to deal with a child, still ventured a word.

"What is thy name, little lass?"

"Gillian," she answered.

"Where's thy home, Gillian?"

"Duck Lane. My father is a carter."

"Have you a garden?"

"Not much. The ducks dig it up."

Simon bought a posy of roses and campion and put it in her hand. Her eyes were dazzled and she was speechless. He looked down at the brown tangles of her hair and thought she looked not much cared for. Then they went on.

By the clogs they found her mother. She was a large woman in a brown cotte, and had a baby on one arm and a basket on the other. When she saw Gillian she put the basket down and gave her a slap, glared at Simon, then seized the basket again and with it drove the little girl before her. Gillian gave one backward look, clutching her posy and weeping, and then she disappeared into the crowd and up St. Martin's Lane. Simon stood like a stranger looking after her. It had happened so quickly, the child engulfed and carried off in her mother's anger, that he was suddenly and unaccountably bereft, like one who had found a jewel, only the next moment to lose it in a swift, black river. But she was only a dirty little girl who was lost; what had come over him, standing openmouthed like a

fool in the middle of market day, and Piers no doubt
making a mucks of things back at the stall. He turned
and went swiftly through the crowd, his face set. He
found Piers in a fluster, some knave having snatched a
pair of red-broidered black gauntlets from under his
very nose, and no sale but a meager one for a small
purse. Simon wordlessly set the stall to rights again,
while Piers snuffled and looked frightened at the un-
toward behavior of his master. He would have felt
more assured had he had a tongue lashing.

Next day being the feast of St. Paul the shop was closed. Restless and ill at ease, Simon paced in the garden. He felt a strange, unreasoning fear growing in him; the night had been sleepless or filled with fitful dreams: Hawise lying dead with Gillian's posy in her hands; the fat Abbot suddenly scuttling crab-like in the old beggar's rags; a mesh bag of cod stinking in the painted coffer when he flung up the lid. By dawn he had been up, and now, as the bells rang merrily from all over town, from the valley, from the far meadows, he had the fowls fed and the cow milked and out to the pasture, and a blank day ahead. Nothing, nothing, nothing. He stopped by the pond to watch the white ducks paddling; eight little ones; with what hawks and turtles would get, maybe there would be three left to fatten for Margrit's oven. He thought of the empty house. He could smell the savory roast in the air—apple, onion, sage—and see the brown, dripping carcass in the platter before him. But none to share it, no one, no one. The fear clutched his throat again. Why? He had been content till now to live in this way. True, he had been joyless, but the days had been full and ever fuller with work for house and homestead and shop; trips to London for the latest goods, the whole enormous pressure of business swallowed him up, the long years of building up respect; Simon Beston, Mercer, bows and curtsies on the streets, and his heart fattening on pride while his soul starved. Now suddenly, frantically, he stopped short before an abyss, like that dream, that doubt which had haunted him intermittently. Was he ill? Was he mad?

He clutched the old willow and watched the ducks paddling around, leaving little spreading ripples behind them that made the reflection of the willow branches dance crazily. He forced his mind to steady. Before that man had come, he asked himself, hadn't everything been as before? Couldn't he go back to before the morning the stranger came, only two days ago, and go on unchanged?

But he could not force his mind back to that time. He had to own that the seed of this unrest had been in him before; man or no man it was there and was only flowering now. But why? What was wrong with his life? He harmed no one; he lived to himself! Ah, but what was right with his life? Was it not barren and void of all but the chink of silver? A cold respect? And a tidy holding? For whom? For himself alone. Alone. But not by his choice, by God's choice who had snatched his wife and child and left him comfortless and cold! God had done this to him! But to how many others? And what did they do? Were they comfortless too? And even those who had not lost wife and child, did they not more often than not curse at one another and beat their children, as Gillian had been beaten?

Gillian. She had looked at him with brown eyes in a smudged face. She had put her hard little hand in his.

She had looked back at him weeping. If he could find her...Duck Lane, she had said. Ah, but what could she matter to him—or he to her? Still, no harm, no harm. At least it was a place to go, a spot to head for, a direction to set his feet and maybe his mind would steady, this turmoil would settle, his eyes would clear, and his world fall into place again.

He left the pond, walked along the path between the wych-elms and went out the garden gate, turning his face toward Duck Lane.

It was past noon when he got there. The town had been merry and full of life. Derek Munsley had caught him near Holy Trinity to tell him that William Fair-cloth, Draper, was selling needle cases and braided belts in his own shop, and was selling kersey and murray in false lengths. Simon had shouldered him off finally to go into St. Martin's for late Mass, which had sickened in his throat. He had come out finally to go into The Falcon across the road, to wash down the whole mess with ale. The Falcon was cool and quiet, and he sat over his tankard in a daze, until a gang came in from the street ribald and noisy and he had pushed himself up, tossed his coin on the table, and made his way out into the blinding sun.

Now he stood just outside Rye Gate, and looked about him. He couldn't remember when he had last been this side of town. Northeast the land sloped off to meadows and marshes lying in the curve of the protecting river; a white gull flashed in the sun and settled on the water. Directly before him down a little path was the Mill, silent today, and beyond it across the river the King's Mead. There was no thoroughfare here; it was quiet after the flurry of the town. Then he looked left along the hovels of Duck Lane—a miserable spot. What had brought him here? What had he hoped from this?

The noon heat of a bright June day lay on the road and hushed the air. He went along slowly. A few dogs came out and barked at him, snapping warily at his heels; he made his way carefully through a little flock of ducks bedraggled and dusty; they scurried to make passage for him. There was a faint smell of cabbage cooking, and a stench of garbage. Most folk were indoors. Smoke rose from a few roofs. There were untidy gardens, the fences knocked awry by the pigs. A thin tethered cow raised its head and looked at him with large, sad eyes. A ragged little boy with a hare-lip stood gaping at him, then ran indoors. A fat woman by one hovel was taking clothes out of a basket to lay them on a hedge to dry. Simon looked at her. It was Gillian's mother.

Then he stopped in his tracks, not knowing what to do. He looked around for Gillian, but there was no one save that fat woman. She had not turned to see him yet. While he stood there in the dust of the road,

Gillian came out of the doorway lugging a pail of swill, and went around the cottage to the pig trough where she dumped it in, the pigs shoving against her skirts and squealing. At the sound the mother turned, and saw him. For a moment she stared at him, and then slowly she remembered; a flush rose on her face, a black look of hatred and fear. She glanced around swiftly, seized a hoe that lay on the ground nearby, and came toward him. He stood dumbstruck and waited till the blows and foul words began to rain upon him.

"Child-snatcher! Lecher! Filthy old man! Get off! Get gone! Do your whoring elsewhere! Hunting out children! Buying them flowers! Spying and prowling! The Devil twist your soul! Get out! Shame and hellfire!"

From the nearby cottages the neighbors ran, seizing stones as they came. Amidst the pain and the hail of words Simon saw Gillian clutching the gate, her little face white, her eyes big with terror, and with all his voice he cried,

"No, Gillian, do not believe her! Do not believe her!" He thought he saw her face change, grow old with understanding and terror of a new sort, and then the hail of stones became too much, and he fled.

Simon had fled up Duck Lane, past Rye Gate, and along the wall where the lane ended in a footpath that hugged the ancient ramparts; he plunged through the thickets and brambles heedlessly, stumbled over refuse heaps, and finally, realizing that he was no longer followed, he sank down and lay there sobbing and panting, surges of pain rising over him. He finally lost consciousness in a kind of stupor. When he stirred himself at last, the shadows of the walls lay over him and halfway down the slope to the meadows; he was cold, sore, thirsty, and filthy. He came to himself slowly, his shocked and battered mind piecing together the cause of his being there. To have been the center and target for the revilings and blows of men—he who had been as withdrawn and secure as a man could be—that mystified him. Also an exhausted peace had hold of him; he was drained of bitterness or vengeance, and had only an acceptance of what he remembered had happened.

He began to wonder dimly what to do, and how to get himself home. It would be long till darkness fell, for the summer twilights were lingering. Anyway, what did he care who saw him; it was only that he felt raw and naked and he dreaded the questioning and shoulderings of men.

He heard a plover crying on the meadow and he could see the people coming and going on East Hill Gate Road and over the meadows and the Lower Mill;

a few boats were on the river, the town lads in them beating the water with their staves and splashing one another; their shouts reached Simon's ears from a great distance. "When the shadows reach the river," he thought, "I will go home."

V

July 22   Feast of St. Mary Magdalen

Rain swept up from the southwest that morning; when he wakened Simon heard it beating on the tiles and dripping off the shutters, and a wind soughed around the house. His first thought was of the Fair, one day old and this the last day, and he felt a fresh sickening at the stench and clamor of it yesterday. Today he would not go.

Slowly he climbed out of bed and went to the press where his clothes hung. He took down an old brown tunic and shook it out. He pulled on his hose and buttoned the tunic with clumsy fingers, for on one thumb there was a festering wound. Margrit would make another poultice for it, he thought, maybe the last it would need. He remembered how the throb of it had wakened him the morning after he had come back from Duck Lane, and he had asked Margrit to bind it up with one of her messes. A bramble or a blow from the hoe must have done the damage. She hadn't asked, and he hadn't said. She'd grumbled at his torn and filthy surcoat, but had not questioned. The bruises on his face had astonished her more no doubt, for he was not one to brawl. But they were gone now.

Rinsing his face in the basin, he wiped it on his sleeve and went down. The kitchen was still dim, but he opened the door to let in the dawn light and the morning air. The wind and rain beat from the other side and he stood looking out at the hives set along the wall between the apple trees; a wren sang out suddenly; the morning was sweet and wet and wild. He laid his head against the doorframe and shut his eyes. What would he make of this day? He would not, he *could* not, go to the Fair, though soon the townfolk would come trooping out at Botolph's Gate, rain or no rain, along the Roman Road past St. Botolph's, and turn off on Magdalen Road down the hill to the Hospital. The last time he had stood so with a blank day before him— it had meant Duck Lane and that sight of Gillian's little face. The pain of that still stung him. Nor could he ever make amends.

If he went away from the Fair, where could he go? Through the town on the other side would mean Duck Lane—not there. The London Road would be crowded. He would go the other way, down More-elm Lane and across the fields to the East Mill and over the river, and then out past the gallows and on the road to Ipswich. Out there, they said, before one came to the road to Wivenhoe, there was a hermit. The hermitage was on a hillside, where there was a tumble of rocks and a big pine. He knew that much from what Derek had said one day, in the Falcon. At least it would be a place to go, a spot to head for, a direction to set his feet.

He turned back into the kitchen. A bottle of mead stood on the table, and a loaf of brown bread. He ate and drank, and then sliced bread and bacon for his wallet. The gusts of rain beat less fitfully against the house now, and he was anxious to be gone. Fastening his belt and pulling his capuchon over his head he went out into the weather, the door swinging to behind him. He went up the path and into the lane; the gate closed behind him with a little click.

About midmorning the sky broke up; in ridges and humps the clouds hurried off eastward before a gay wind; the sunlight fell in shafts over the hills and then came out fully except where the black cloud shadows sailed slowly over field and woodland. By noon Simon sank in the grass by the roadside and took out his wallet; he felt hungry and weary. When he had eaten he rolled over and looked about him. There was an immense silence over everything, and he lay in a sort of hollow in the land, before the muddy track went over a little rise and skirted the beech woods. There was red clover all about him sweet-smelling and bee-swarming, and by a stone a slender plant with sturdy blue flowers, succory; he had seen it many times, yet his eye fastened on it now and his mind circled around a memory and finally came to rest on that other blue flower, sewn on the man's tunic: blue and round like this one, but cupped like a buttercup, blue-veined gold in the center, with three black stamens tipped with gold. He was amazed at how he remembered it; and he stared now at this flower, wondering dully where the other flower grew and if he could ever find it, and why a man would ever travel anyway except on pilgrimage to save his soul, or if one was driven to it by poverty or sin, or by some desperate quest.

He watched a hawk coasting around and around far up, and wondered if it spied him with its sharp eyes, an unaccustomed lump here by the roadside. A cricket clambered through the grass near his hand. "Bird and bug and man," he thought. "Peace and naught else. What if I should come to that, like the hermit." Then he roused himself and stood up; around the curve of the woods he thought, and up on the hill, beyond which lay the forest of Wivenhoe, there was the hermit. He stooped and plucked a flower of succory, thrusting it in his tunic, and then he went on up the road.

When he reached the bend in the road he saw the great pine on the hillside, saplings and jumbled rocks at its foot, and a tiny hut. He stood and watched for a moment; there was no movement about the place except for a thin trail of smoke. What to do next? He had heard it often said that people came to see the hermit. Derek's wife had brought their sick baby here and afterward it thrived. It was said by some he was a wizard and by others he was holy and by others that he was mad. "He may be all three," thought Simon, and began to climb the hill. As he came nearer he called out, "Father, Father," and waited; then he called again. This time the skins over the door parted and an old man peered out; when he saw Simon he slowly came forth. He was bent, grizzled, in a ragged brown robe.

"A blessing, Father," called Simon, and the old man made the sign of the cross in the air before him. Simon drew nearer. Now, he could see the old man's eyes, very black, with red rims, and his toothless mouth.

"What is it ye seek, son?" he asked, looking at Simon with an unchanged face.

"Peace from torment," said Simon.

"What is thy torment?"

Ah, what *was* his torment!

"I am of all men alone, and I have a great emptiness, within me and beneath."

The old man still stood motionless and pondering.

"To be single and alone is good; only so are men not trapped into sin."

"Is that God's will?"

"Yea."

There was a silence between them. Then Simon with that ache in his breast said, "What of the emptiness?"

"Fill thyself with God."

"How can I? How can I?"

"Forswear thy fellowman, stamp out Adam. Leave the foul world."

Simon stared at him, the crumpled face, the sharp eyes.

"Father, is there no other purpose, no comfort?"

"None."

Simon slowly shook his head; he felt rising in him a tide of refusal; the words No, no, no! surged up in him, but he throttled them at the sight of that pitiable face, those tattered shoulders. Then he turned and plunged down the hillside, fleeing as he had fled Duck Lane, and he ran until he was around the curve of the road again. Then he slowed, panting. When he passed his former resting place he saw the succory, blue and sturdy, by the stone, and he looked at the flower in his tunic: it was limp and grey, all color drained from it.

VI

August 24

Simon had taken a day from the shop to bring in the hay from the lower meadow; with Piers he had worked long in the sun. Far off he could see the Bishop's Fields of wheat, bright orange and a dull gold where great cloud shadows drifted over them; another day or two and they would be laid low and gathered in, the great stooks standing in rows. It would be a good harvest. Now he went to the well and splashed water over his face and arms, and then flung himself down by the shrunken duck pond. The wych-elm leaves hung dusty and still. The ricks that had been empty were full now, by the cow shed, and Piers clambered about pitching the last sheaves in. The shadows lay long across the grass and the cropping sheep. It was cooler but the air was pent; a haze of midges danced before his eyes and he brushed them away. Margrit tossed a basin of water out the buttery door; it fell in a silvery shower. Near at hand and clear in the still air the passing bell began to toll at St. Botolph's. Simon listened, and ran over in his mind who was ill or dying in the parish, then he sat up. It rang the three times three strokes for a man, and then the heavy, steady toll of years.

"Piers."

Piers turned his head and stopped his work.

"Piers, the bell. For whom does it ring?"

Piers shook his head dumbly. Simon had lost count of the strokes, but it was for no youth. Margrit came to the buttery door again and stood listening.

"Mayhap for that Poor Priest that came through yesterday," she said. "He was taken with a falling fit and they shrived him last night."

"Where did they take him?"

"Priest Fulcun had him, though not gladly."

The bell ceased. Simon lay back. Margrit called the hens and clucked at them, scattering corn; then she went in. He lay for a long time and thought of a man dying a stranger and unwanted; and for what he came there in the parish only to be smitten dumb. He had heard these men preached poverty and simple truth, whatever that was, and made the bishops squirm. Also that they had the word of Scripture changed into English, for any man to read. But the man was dead now, thought Simon, and would have no more words, but would be laid unknown in the parish field.

Then Simon sat up, going suddenly dizzy; he laid his head on his knees and waited till his mind steadied. No harm to go, and ask for him at least; though he'd heard of them he'd seen no Poor Priest yet; he might as well look on a dead one who could not stir him with the words that would give a fruitless hope.

137

In the long dusk he went down through the meadow and across the field into the churchyard. The evening was sweet now; swallows skimmed the grasses and a nighthawk cried as it wheeled above the tower; there was the scent of phlox, and mown hay, and crushed mint. As he went in by the porch a bat flittered out mewing softly, and was gone in the shadows. The church was dark and cool; in the chancel the candles winked and gleamed, and the great chalice shimmered. But there was no bier, so he went softly across to Our Lady's Chapel on the north side. There in the dim light he saw the bier, candles at head and feet, and a figure kneeling before the rood. He went forward slowly until, in the light that flickered at his step, he looked at the body of the dead priest. He was old, yet not so old, with weathered face, a beaked nose, and two lines cut deep in his cheeks; his hands were folded on a wooden cross, and he was clad in a russet gown, the hood folded back under his head; the mud of the road was still on the hem. They had taken off his sandals. And his feet... "Ah," thought Simon, "they could not even wash his feet," and a little knot came in his throat.

The figure kneeling by the rood stirred and rose haltingly, with mutterings and groans; the man shuffled forward and gave a start to find Simon standing there motionless. It was Priest Fulcun's vicar, Father Meurice.

"Comst tha to watch?" he hissed.

Simon shook his head.

"Knows tha his name?" asked the vicar.

"Nay. I only heard there was a man died here."

"Peace to him. There's some of his kind would get no decent burial, what with their preaching and dissension. Fulcun was rare put to it to know what to do with this un." And Meurice chuckled a little, glad of a bit of company.

"Said he nought before he took sick?" asked Simon, his eyes on the still face in the wavering light.

"Nay. They found him by Shire Gate, all in a heap, and brought him here, knowing the Abbey would have nought to do with him. He had a great book with him, which Fulcun tossed with the rubbish to be burned. We'll send a missive to Lutterworth tomorrow—where this kind comes from—and doubtless they'll know which of 'em it is, but he'll be in the ground before they get here, if they come."

There was a silence, except for a faint sputter of candle and the breathing of the two men. Simon went on his knees beside the bier; but he could not pray; even the Pater Noster had gone clean out of his head;

so he knelt there wordless and empty for a seemly interval, and then he stumbled to his feet and went out.

On the porch he paused, one hand resting on the cool stone. Daylight had gone now. Something stayed his feet. Where was the rubbish heap? He searched his memory. It would be around behind Fulcun's house, where the covered walk led to the little door and gallery stair; there in the corner he had seen a jumble of trash, hidden by hollyhocks. He slipped out into the dark and around the church, cursing the dim light yet glad that it covered him. He felt grass under his feet and the stones of the wall under his fingers, and at length ivy, and thick furry leaves on thick stalks; then he went down on his knees, feeling a prick of broken glass, a moldy vestment, and at last a leather binding; he tugged at it, and the book came into his hands. He stood up in the dark, clasping it, and listening. Nothing stirred but the glitter of stars above him and a little wind. Then he went off noiselessly, through the dim yard, across the meadow, and into his own land.

The house was dark, for Margrit had gone home. On the kitchen hearth the fire was carefully covered. He laid the book on the table, took a fat beeswax candle from the cupboard, and knelt to light it from the embers; then he rose and set it on the table. In the ring of yellow light he saw the book for the first time, a plain brown leather cover which he unclasped and laid back, and saw the thick pages covered with neat, close rows of letters. He drew up a stool, pulled the candle closer, and, laying elbows on the table, he began to read.

At the first cockcrow, he raised his head. The candle had burned down to within an inch of its socket. His eyes smarted and his shoulders ached; his mouth was dry. Rising stiffly, he rummaged on the shelf for mead, and poured a tankard, which he drank standing, with his eyes closed and his head swimming. Then he set the tankard down and began to walk softly back and forth, back and forth, before the hearth. He felt empty and light, shattered and unchained. At last he stopped, and gripped the edge of the table, and muttered between his teeth.

"It was all false, from the day I came forth and was christened until now. It was all false and falsehood. I never knew God or God's Son. I was fed shame and lies and tricks and mumblings, bowings and mysteries, a ladder of priests and false holiness up to the Holy Father himself, and preachings of Heaven and Hell that gold could buy, or buy pardon and blessedness. I wipe it all out; I cast it all away. I know naught. I am naked as the day I was born. Now I must find out. I must find what God is and who is his Son, and what he wants of me, if he is at all."

Then he sank down on the stool again and hunted for words that hammered at his mind; when he found them, he pulled the candle closer and read again, his fingers running over the page.

"And he said, A man hadde twei sonses; and the younger of hem seide to the fadir, Fadir, gyue me the porcioun of catel, that fallith to me. And he departid to hem the catel. And not after many days, when all things were gathered together, the younger son went forth in pilgrimage in to a far country; and there he wasted his goods in living lecherously. And after that he had ended all things, a strong hunger was made in that country, and he began to have need. And he went and drew him to one of the citizens of that country. And he sent him into his town, to feed swine. And he coveted to fill his womb of the cods that the hogs eat, and no man gave him. And he turned again to himself, and said, How many hired men in my father's house have plenty of loaves; and I perish here through hunger. I shall rise up, and I shall go to my father, and I shall say to him, Father I have sinned in to heaven, and before thee; and now I am not worthy to be clept thy son, make me as one of thy hired men. And he rose up, and came to his father. And when he was yet afar, his father saw him, and was stirred by mercy. And he ran, and fell on his neck, and kissed him. And the son said to him, Father, I have sinned in to heaven, and before thee,

and now I am not worthy to be clept thy son. And the father said to his servants, Swithe bring ye forth the first stool and clothe ye him and give ye a ring in his hand, and shoon on his feet; and bring ye a fat calf, and slay ye, and eat we, and make we feast. For this my son was dead, and he has lived again; he perished, and is found. And all men begun to eat. But his elder son was in the field; and when he came and nighed to the house, he heard a symphony and a crowd. And he clept one of the servants, and asked, what these things were. And he said to him, Thy brother is come, and thy father slew a fat calf, for he received him safe. And he was wroth, and would not come in. Therefore his father went out, and began to pray him. And he answered to his father and said, Lo! so many years I serve thee, and I never brake thy commandment; and thou never gave to me a kid, that I with my friends should have eaten. But after that this thy son, that hath devoured his substance with whores, came, thou hast slain to him a fat calf. And he said to him, Son, thou art ever more with me, and all my things be thine. But it behoved for to make feast, and to have joy; for this thy brother was dead, and lived again; he perished, and is found."

The candle all but winked out. He rose hurriedly and fetched another, conscious of the day soon coming, and Margrit finding him there before long. He set wick to wick and watched the new wick flare, and in the fresh light hunted farther.

"If I speak with the tongues of men and of angels, and I have not charity, I am made as brass sounding or a cymbal tinkling. And if I have prophecy, and know all mysteries and all cunning, and if I have all faith, so that I move hills from their place, and I have not charity, I am naught. And if I depart all my goods in to the meats of poor men, and if I betake my body, so that I burn, and if I have not charity, it profiteth to me nothing. Charity is patient, it is benign; charity envieth not, it doeth not wickedly, it is not upblown, it is not covetous, to seeketh not the things that be its own, it is not stirred to wrath, it thinketh not evil, it joyeth not on wickedness, but it joyeth together to truth; it suffereth all things, it believeth all things, it hopeth all things, it sustaineth all things. Charity falleth never down, whether prophecies shall be void, or languages shall cease, or science shall be destroyed. For a part we know; and a part we prophesy; but when that shall come which is perfect, that thing that is of part shall be avoided. When I was a little child, I spake as a little child, I understood as a little child; but when I was made a man, I avoided the things that were of a little child. And we see now by a mirror in darkness, but then face to face; now I know of part, but then I shall know, as I am known. And now dwell faith, hope, charity, these three; but the most of these is charity."

He sank back, with his hands over his face. Then he leaned forward again slowly, and this time sought in John.

"And in one day of the week Mary Magdalene came early to the grave, when it was yet dark. And she saw the stone moved away from the grave. There she ran, and came to Simon Peter, and to another disciple, whom Jesus loved, and saith to them, They have taken the Lord from the grave, and we wis not where they have laid him. Therefore Peter went out, and that other disciple, and they came to the grave. And they twain run together, and that other disciple run before Peter, and came first to the grave. And when he stooped, he saw the sheets lying, natheless he entered not. Therefore Simon Peter came pursuing him, and he entered in to the grave and he saw the sheets laid, and the napkin that was on his head, not laid with the sheets but by itself wrapped in to a place. Therefore that disciple that came first to the grave, entered and saw and believed. For they knew not yet the scripture, that it behoved him to rise again from death. Therefore the disciples went eftsoon to themselves. But Mary stood at the grave with outforth weeping. And the while she wept, she bowed her, and beheld forth in to the grave. And she saw two angels sitting in white, one at the head and one at the feet, where to body of Jesus was laid. And they said to her, Woman, what weepest thou?

She said to them, For they have taken away my Lord, and I wot not where they have laid him. When she said these things, she turned backward, and saw Jesus standing, and wist not that it was Jesus. Jesus saith to her, Woman, what weepest thou? Whom seekest thou? She guessing that it was the gardener, saith to him, Sire, if thou hast taken him up, say to me where thou hast laid him, and I shall take him away. Jesus saith to her, Mary. She turned and saith to him, Raboni, that is to say, Master. Jesus saith to her, Nill thou touch me, for I have not yet ascended to my Father; but go to my brethren and say to them, I go to my Father, to my God, and to your God. Mary Magdalene came, telling to the disciples that I saw the Lord, and these things He said to me. Therefore when it was eve in that day, one of the sabbaths, and the gates were shut, where the disciples were gathered, for dread of the Jews, Jesus came, and stood in the middle of the disciples, and he saith to them, Peace to you. And when he had said this, he showed to them hands and side; therefore the disciples joyed, for the Lord was seen. And he saith to them eftsoons, Peace to you: as the Father sent me, I sent you. When he has said this, he blew on them, and said, Take ye the Holy Ghost; whose sins ye forgive, they be forgiven to them; and whose ye withhold, they be withholden. But Thomas, one of the twelve, that is said Didymus, was not with them when Jesus came.

Therefore the other disciples said, We have seen the Lord. And he said to them, But I see in his hands the print of nails and put my hand into his side, I shall not believe. And after eight days eftsoon his disciples were with in, and Thomas with them. Jesus came, while the gates were shut, and stood in the middle, and said, Peace to you. Afterward he saith to Thomas, Put here thy finger, and see mine hands, and put hither thine hand, and put into my side, and nil thou be unbelieveful, but faithful. Thomas answered and said to him, My Lord and my God. Jesus saith to him, Thomas, for thou hast seen me, thou believedest; blessed be they that see not, and have believed. And Jesus did many other signs in the sight of his disciples, which be not written down in this book. But these be written, that ye believe, that Jesus is Christ, the son of God, and that ye believing have life in his name."

"... ye believing have life in his name," he whispered. His face was drawn and old, and his fingers shook. Dimly he heard the cock crow again, and the sleepy hens begin to call. He rose, snuffing the candle and shutting the book with a little thud. He carried the book through the shop into the hall, where he hid it in the great chest, under his furred cloak. Then he came back to tidy the kitchen, and flung open the door to let in the morning. A robin sat by the well, and flew up as he came out to draw water. He doused his head and his eyes began to clear a bit; the drops clung to his brows and his beard. Then he leaned against the rim and looked off across the meadows to where St. Botolph's spire rose above the churchyard. They would be burying the Poor Priest this morning. They would be burying Simon, too, all that he had known or thought or, unheeding, had believed. He no longer questioned if it was false; he knew. But what was true, or what lay beyond him—emptiness or life—or what he must do—that he did not know.

VII

September 23

The haze of autumn lay on the land; the evenings had a chill, and the call of the rooks a wintry sound, as they flapped in a straggling line homeward in the shortening twilight. The harvest was in but the fields not empty, for the ploughmen were out again, and sowing winter wheat and rye. The colors and sounds of the earth were changed. Simon's garden was full of roses. The herbs were cut and hung in the kitchen to dry. The apple trees were heavy laden, and Margrit heard all day as she worked the plunk of apples falling to the grass. The straw hives had been carefully lifted and robbed of a portion of their combs. The onions were pulled and hung in strings from the rafters.

After the long, warm, growing days of summer, it was a time of gathering and drawing in, of laying up for the dark, cold days ahead. Winters had been hard of late years; snows had been deep and the storms fierce, with wicked tides on the coasts, and lowlands flooded. People had starved, and more than one traveler had vanished to be found in the spring thaws a heap of rags in a snowdrift. Winter was an evil thing if one was not ready for it. So Margrit and Piers labored as usual. But Simon went about with a set face doing the accustomed tasks only in a heartless way, and often went off without a word to be gone all day, and they did not know where he was or why he had gone. People had begun to look at him in the town and mutter about him. Something was not right. The Priest Fulcun had stopped him in the street once, and fixed him with his eye, and uttered a pious phrase, but Simon had stared at him as if he were not there, and pushed on.

Simon was empty and lost. Each dawn was a fresh dread; each day must be labored through, and each night a time of torment, when he lay in the dark silence and looked into the abyss. The ingathering of summer, the mellow colors of the autumn earth, the song of the ploughman to his oxen, drifting over the hedgerows, the whirr and wheel of the clouds of swallows as they circled and dipped in the clear air, they stirred his heart with a terrible ache. He was not fit to share in creation with such beauty. Of all God's creatures man was the foulest and the most perverse, the most alone for all his society; and he, Simon, was of all men the most perverse—though many of the sins preached against he had not done in fact. But in his heart he had done them all, and a deep-rooted, all-pervading, subtle sin had overwhelmed him; he lay in its clutches, recognizing it yet unable to be free: the sin of denial to life, loveless, coldhearted, deaf and blind to God, hedged in by self, lost in a maze, trustless.

Now, on this fair and ingathering day, with a frosty sparkle in the air, he closed the stall early, gathered the wares and all their gear into a barrow, and sent Piers off with it alone. Then he went slowly through the town, looking at faces, listening to voices. He felt odd and disembodied, almost as if he were not in his flesh there, and truly it seemed as if no one saw him, and he walked invisible. It was only when a rough shoulder brushed him, or a man with a cart shouted him out of the way, that he knew he was there and not in a dream.

So, as the bells of the Abbey rang for Evensong and the bells of Trinity echoed them, he drifted into the Falcon, where a fire already snapped and hissed on the hearth against the chill and the dim light. A row of pewter tankards glowed on the shelf. From the pantry there came the tuneless hum of the alewife at her work. The place was empty, except for a small cluster in the corner of men he did not know—a carter, a ploughman, a chapman with a dark, wild face, and a forester in green. Simon slipped into a settle nearby and signaled for ale, then he stared into the fire, his eyes blurred and his mind dumb.

After a long while the voices reached him.

"I met him north, towards Cantebrege, on the far side of the forest, where the track runs into the road to Bery. I've met many a man for talk in my day, but none like him. I took him home to Nan that night, but she'd have none of it, turned him out next morning, and bid me settle my thoughts and stick to my green." It was the forester talking. "Women are always fearful for house and hearth and what might threaten it. But his words run in my mind still."

"What manner of talk? Priest or friar? Stirring the Commons?"

"Nay, not that." The forester sighed and was silent, as if listening within. "It was as if, as if he came from another land, and strove to tell me of it, a fair land, full of peace. He said there was no man there who did not belong, and they belonged to one another. He said men should belong to one another, not going each his own way but shoulder to shoulder following the same master. He said God meant us to be one, and to be joyful."

The chapman pushed his mug aside and laughed. "Joyful? Should we laugh at the pestilence and chuckle at an empty belly, and be glad over a cruel master?"

"Aye, I asked him that. He said God suffered with us in our pain, and held us in the hollow of his hand no matter what the world might deal us, and in him and one another we might have joy despite all. But mostly God suffers for our heartlessness, and because we do not see that we are his and one another's."

There was a short silence, marked by the thump of ale mugs and shifting of feet.

"Where was he from and what was his trade?"

"A shepherd. He did not rightly say where his city was—north, and west, over the hills. Nor shall I ever see it, if it is at all. A man can dream of such a place—but he is bound to his spot of earth and tied as tight as ever was bondsman tied, and no year and a day can free him from the yoke of this life into a free city of such love as this shepherd spoke. Still and all . . . if it is God's will we live in such love . . . then in what sin do we all stew . . . and should not all chains be brast apart though we die for it!...I know not, I know not. Only his words come back to me now and again, and I would Nan had heeded him also."

"Men ever dream such things and they come to naught," said the carter, uneasily. "Such idle talk leads us away from what we are duty bound to follow, here and now. The snares and pitfalls ye'll find in the forest are such sins as should trouble you. Leave the rest to priest and bishop!"

"Mayhap," groaned the forester. He pushed back his empty flagon and they all rose. There was the rattle and ring of coin and the stamping of feet. As they reached the door Simon found himself by the forester, his hand clutched on his green sleeve. He pulled him aside.

"Tell me," he whispered, "where wast ye saw this man, and how long past?"

The forester looked at him with sad, black eyes in a seamed face. "A fortnight gone. By the road to Bery. He went toward Cantebrege," he said.

"Had he a blue flower broidered here?" and Simon's hand went to his breast, where the pain was.

"Aye, now I think of it, he did. Knowst him also?"

"Him or his brother. And I die at the roots—we all die at the roots—for lack of that ground in which he dwells."

The two men stared at one another; the look went deep, in it the knowledge of all need, a far-reaching, naked knowledge past all words.

"I go," gasped Simon. "I needs must, though I die in it."

And then the chapman broke upon them with his wild laugh, a hand on each man's shoulder pushing them apart. "Come, man, we are late now at Martin's house and his good wife will scold. Supper waits and this idle talk addles your wits." He pulled the forester into the street. Simon turned blindly toward home, running. The pain round his heart spread but he did not heed it, nor anything but the hammering in his brain. He was going, going. He was a fool, but God's fool at least. If he could do naught else he could be God's fool. And so he ran.

Darkness found him in the kitchen, writing slowly and painfully. He laid down his quill and stared at his words.

The Secret Flower

*I, Simon Beston, am leaving this life. All that
is in this shop should be sold at fair price and
the monies given to the poor of this parish.
House and land is for Margrit Goodspeed and
her son Piers. May God have mercy on us all.*

Then he rose. He went through the shop and into
the hall to the great carved chest. He took out his
furred cloak, and the great book. This he carried
out to the well, where he dropped it in, waiting till
the splash had died away and the water settled. Then
he went back in, to the kitchen, with the cloak over
his arm. This he laid on the bench while he packed
his wallet with bread and cheese. The keys from the
chain at his belt he took off and laid on the paper
he had written. Then he stood for a moment looking
about him, before he picked up the flickering candle
and blew it out. In the blackness he gathered up his
cloak and felt his way to the door. Outside, it was
cool and dark. Ben, tied by the apple tree, rose, growl-
ing faintly in his throat. Simon touched his head, and
the stiff, upstanding ears. Then he went down the
path and pushed open the gate, letting it click to
behind him. Then he set his feet toward the London
Road, and Cantebrege.

PART TWO

I

October 24   Feast of Edward the Confessor

The forest was still when Simon halted, and full
of rustle when he went ahead, for the track was all
but hidden by the fallen leaves. Once he came upon
pigs rooting for mast in the soft earth under the oaks,
and they went squealing into the underbrush; and
in a clearing where the grass was still fair and green
a herd of wild ponies was cropping; they, too, lit off
at his step and he listened to the light thunder of their
hoofs until they stopped, waiting for him to move on.
The sun came through in great patches where the
leaves were already down, and in patterns of light
and shade where the late leaves hung still on the ash
trees and the grey beeches. A squirrel leapt along a
branch. With a whirr of wings a partridge flew up
out of the brake. But there was no man save Simon,
who was enveloped in a great peace.

He had left Braintree at dawn, making toward
Walden, he hoped, and then on toward Cantebrege
which was still several days' journey away at the
pace he took. The tentative questions he had put about
the man had been met with blank looks. Folk had
been friendly enough. He had worked in the harvest

a day here, a day there, to refill his wallet. The fair weather had held. He was weary, and the pain around his heart persisted but he went ahead. He thought of Gillian now and again, and the forester, and once or twice of Margrit hoping she had met with no trouble after he had gone. But it was as if house and shop and all the trappings of his former life had vanished away.

Only he found Hawise in his thoughts more than ever at any time since her death; even her face came before him vivid and clear again; he dreamed of her at night and her persistent presence followed him all day. Something or someone he had once tried to blank out of his life and dismiss as meaningless now entered in afresh; fear of pain at remembering had disappeared and he welcomed Hawise now. He thought of her as he walked, with a feeling so strange to him that he did not know that it was joy. Once as he went through a clearing in the early morning he gathered a few asters for her, and carried them all day, half expecting to come across her as he walked; in the evening when they were wilted and pale he laid them under a little aspen tree whose leaves were all atremble, and he went on, feeling tears upon his cheeks. It was a mystery, that he carried Hawise in his heart now, when she had been, he supposed, forgotten; and by virtue of his lovelessness and forgetting, surely she had long since withdrawn from him; but no, she was there. He dreamed of her as she first came into his uncle's shop, in a scarlet

hood, to buy needles, and he had pricked his fingers
when he had showed them to her, so awestruck he was
by her green eyes and the freckles on her nose, and
her slender fingers that held the needles up to the light
one by one. And then he had met her when he had gone
a-maying; and they had walked in the lanes, in that
wild, sweet spring. And he remembered now her care
of him, for no wish of his that she could fill had ever
gone unanswered.

He thought of himself very little now, of his plight
or any danger and discomfort he might be in. His
heart had been split wide open. He saw everything;
the bug colored and shaped like a knight's shield on
the wild crabapple where he stopped to eat; the hare
that sat up in the long grass and looked at him; the
sweeping frond of fern all spotted in even rows of
velvet brown on the underside; the sleek otter sliding
into the water of the black forest pool. He felt, too,
for all he met: the leper on the far side of Waltham
who had gone off into a field to wait for Simon to
pass, standing like an eyeless statue in his hood and
wide hat and black cloak, his clapper clutched to his
side; the goose girl singing to her flock as she went
down the hillside to the stream; the Earl's men riding
in from the forest with three dead deer lashed on poles
slung between their horses, the laughing and the loud
words, the bright tunics and heraldry. Pictures hung
in his mind as on a tapestry. It was as if he had never

seen the world before—God's world or the men in it.

Now he went through the woods arustle at his step. Past midday a little breeze sprang up; he could hear it in the treetops overhead. The sunlight grew more golden and warm, and he grew wearier. The track went down a gradual slope, into a clearing, and in the middle stood a great beech, still holding all its leaves. He made for it, thinking to rest beneath it, striding down through the long grass with the crickets leaping aside at his step, to where ponies had cropped the grass short all around the tree; and there he stood in a dazzle, for the breeze blew up again, but strongly now, and as he stood the leaves began to fall. They were steady and golden in a great shower as the tree took the wind; on and on they fell, as if his coming had been a signal for their descent, and as if his stepping out of the circle would signal them to stop. He stood there amazed, with leaves on his head and shoulders and brushing his cheek and falling all around him like golden snow; for long moments they fell, and when the wind at last passed on, the tree was nearly bare; and a few last leaves spun down; the soft, magical music floated away; Simon stood ankle deep in gold, with the golden sunlight pouring down upon him.

Out of the past there came to him another time when he had stood ankle deep in gold with sunlight warm upon him; but the gold had been buttercups, and he

was a little lad running in from a long morning in
the June hay harvest, and at the edge of the meadow
he had met his mother, a tall lady in a blue gown; she
had caught him and knelt before him, with a hand
upon each shoulder, and she had smiled into his eyes,
with a look of joy upon her face. "Little son," she
had said, "the sunshine has already kissed thee on
thy nose but mayhap thy chin is left for me!" And
she had ducked him a kiss upon his chin, and then
let him run laughing off to the well to wash before
his meal. He remembered the plash of water on his
face, and the look of her still standing there watching
him.

Soon after that she had suddenly died, and his
dark, silent father had sent him off to the Abbey to
get some schooling, as he had a sweet voice and a
musical ear and a keen mind for learning. So the
cold stone had begun to close around him, and at
twelve, with no heart for the life of the Church or
for much else either, he had left the Abbey and gone
into his uncle's shop, with a firm ground of learning
and sums and a guarded heart. And until this moment
he had hardly thought of her.

Now in an instant she had been given back to him.
He was a little lad again and her joy in his small
manliness stood like a shield between him and all
sorrow. He felt as if his heart would break with a
new amazement. Like long-forgotten treasure poured

into his lap, love flooded him. He had cried out against God for having denied him love, but now he knew it had been there and was there and had always followed him but his blindness and stoniness had shut it out. Even with Hawise he had not rightly known the gem that had lain in his hands—even for so brief a time. Like jewels upon a necklace he counted now the remembered times love had been proffered him. God had loved him, had poured out love upon him, had given him the gift over and over again, but he had not recognised or remembered; his ingratitude had clouded all his sight; he it was who had been loveless, not God, whose ways were past question.

So he wept, standing under the leafless beech, with sorrow for the past but joy for the present; then in weakness he sank down among the fallen leaves and put his back against the warm tree, and set his mind, with a kind of wondering courage, toward the future, and after a while in gratitude he fell asleep.

II

November 24   Leicester

The pale winter sun shone on the great courtyard astir and noisy. Through the wide gates haywains rumbled, dogs barking by the wheels, carters shouting, urchins catching at the straw that hung over the wain sides and left a trail on the cobbles. Maids carried green rushes from a laden wagon into the new church to strew on the stone floor, and came out laughing and singing for more armfuls. A dozen sheep were driven slowly through the hurrying press, toward the kitchen and offices and kitchen yard; and three peasants came lurching through with reed pens of squawking hens on their backs, headed the same way. A cool wind blew in from the river, and tossed the sound of the new organ from the new church in billows on the air. From the ancient parish chapel the bell pealed and the pigeons scattered in alarm, circling the grey Norman towers, swinging free over the river and the brown oaks on the other shore, circling back, and settling again to strut and mutter on the walls.

The whole castle, the whole town was out and busy, for the Earl of Lancaster himself was coming. The new church, St. Mary in the Newark, was being blessed by the Bishop, and under its stones the Earl himself would sometime lie, and all his descendants. Now in the thin November chill the people forgot the season that lay ahead, the long dark and the cold, and made a merry stir.

As the last wain rolled in the Steward's man checked it off and shouted to clear a passage for it while the great, meek oxen with their massive heads and swinging shoulders plodded steadily toward the wide-flung doors of the Hall. The man on the top of the load dug his fork into a toppling corner of the hay and braced with his feet as they rocked to a halt. He gritted his teeth as pain across his chest and shoulders spread, and his eyes swam. A shout from below—"Holla, man! Toss it down!" roused him and his eyes cleared. Simon, for it was he, let the first load of straw slide down with a rustling thud onto the threshold, and the Earl's men with their forks tossed it bundle by bundle into the sweet duskiness of the Hall. As he stooped to pitch a load down he glimpsed within the huge oaken pillars, the great dais at the far end, and the wide hearth. Then he forgot all in the steady labor, the pitch and toss, pitch and toss, until the wain was bare except for stubble and chaff, and he could clamber down, sweating and dizzy. The Steward's man hastened by.

"Quench your thirst in the kitchen yard, man," he

said, not unkindly, as he saw Simon's white face. " 'Tis yonder"— pointing to a huddle of outbuildings that flanked the Hall under the wall on the right. Then he hurried on. Simon looked across at the kitchen; the distance between seemed like a vast sea of rippling cobbles, but he set his feet that way. He had all but reached the other side when the pain seized him again; this time it could not be denied. He staggered to the low wall of the kitchen garden and clung there, panting. The carter who had driven Simon's wagon in came out of the door with a tankard in his hand; he set it down on the sill with a cry and sprang forward, as for Simon the world went black and roaring, and then still.

Dancing firelight was the first thing he saw; out of a deep and terrible sense of loss and despair he began to struggle, like a swimmer fighting toward the surface with bursting lungs. The faint firelight beckoned, and he knew he had not died. Shimmering and gleaming like treasure the knowledge came that he had not died and he yet could journey on his search; God had put life back in his hands, it was not finished!

There was no more pain, only a terrible weakness that was iron on all his limbs. When he opened his eyes again, he saw a man's face bending over him—the eyes, one was black and bright, the other cloudy and blind with a deep scar behind it. The man smiled; he had broken teeth, and pox, but he looked kind.

"Well," he said. "We near called the priest for ye, but maybe ye'll do after all. A little broth now'll set the blood astir again."

He lifted Simon's head gently and put a cup to his lips. The broth was tasty and strong. Simon took a small sip, and then a longer. The man laid him back, and sat looking at him.

"In time," he said, "tell who ye are and from where, for you're not much known in these parts. This is St. Edmund's Hospice and Almshouse, and I am the Warden. The Carter from Kirby Manor brought ye here after he'd picked ye up in a fit at the Castle. Said ye'd come from the road to the east a fortnight gone, looking for work, and he called ye Simon. But now rest and sleep."

Out of a spinning and shattered world pieces began to slip in place; Simon kept his eyes fixed on the man's face. The thought went on dancing in his mind like a gem. "Maybe I shall yet find it; I am not yet dead. God still gives me life."

"More broth," he whispered.

"Easy, man, easy," said the Warden. "Thee'll have plenty of time for eating. 'Tis peaceful now with all gone to the great feast at the Castle. I stayed by to watch, not knowing whether ye'd be a corpse soon or begin to draw breath more easily. Now methinks ye'll do, with rest, and food, and drink, and a bit of this brew —made from the foxglove I grew in our own garden." He rose and fetched more wood for the fire, and from a hutch near the hearth he poured a drink from a small blue jug into an earthenware mug. This he brought to Simon. But first he knelt and laid a finger on Simon's wrist, feeling the heartbeats, with his shrewd black eye on Simon's face.

"Now drink this, man, and then sleep."

The drink was bitter and cool. Simon lay back, spent and weaker than a babe; out of a sick weakness and a new joy, tears gathered in the corners of his eyes and slid down his cheeks. The Warden, stooping to cover him, tched with his tongue.

"What do ye weep for now, man?"

"Out of joy . . . that I have not died," whispered Simon.

The Warden sat on a low stool by Simon's pallet. He fixed his eye again on Simon's face.

" 'Tis many a mortal would weep because they had

not died, and only because God has given them a certain span do they go on pushing and plodding. Is the world that gay? Or thy good fortune so great? Thee pricks me with a wonder, man. Yet 'tis no time to ply thee with talk! Here I tell thee to sleep, and then sit chinning." His black eye winked. "In the morning after the beggars and poor wanderers have guzzled their porridge and gone out on the streets, then thee can better talk, and I can listen."

Simon closed his eyes. He saw in his mind's eye the old beggars he had seen often on Colchester Market, the old man who had begged of the Abbot the day he met Gillian, and the paupers, the poor wandering landless men, whom he had scorned, not pitied, and hounded, not loved. And now here he lay—weak, penniless—yet joy played over him and warmed his limbs like the firelight. And then he slept.

He slept so long and so sound, he never heard or saw the rabble that crept in as night settled, nor the Warden hushing them and shaking his fist at them if they began to jest and raise a ruckus, nor how one or two came to cast a look at him, and then went to their own pallets to lie down groaning and stretching till sleep took them. He could not know that all that night the Warden sat by him, with an eye on his breathing, and a finger laid now and again on his wrist, and now and again rising to stir up the fire. And yet, also, he did know it, for love warmed his limbs, and love beat quietly and strongly in his pulse and laid peace on his mind.

As morning came he woke when the Warden's man came through ringing a little bell and rousing all the poor. They rose yawning and scratching and groaning from their beds and trooped noisily out of the long dormitory into the room beyond. Through the wide stone doorway Simon could see, from where he lay, a long table, with benches, and bowls set out, and the Warden standing over a huge steaming pot of porridge. He filled each bowl with a dripping ladle, and bade them sit, and then a long lean priest came in, and blessed them all, and mumbled a prayer. Then they all began to eat, spoons scraping the bowls, a low mumble of talk, coughs, clearing of throats, here and there a long sigh. Simon heard the priest say to the Warden:

"Where is the sick man brought in last night?"

With averted face, busy with stirring up the porridge, the Warden answered, "Still sleeping. He is mending now."

So the priest went away. And Simon fell into a doze again. When he woke the place was quiet. The Warden sat near the fire, a stool pulled up to a low table, working his accounts in a large ledger. Simon watched him for a bit. Then he said softly, "I would I could pay thee a bit for all thy care for me."

The Warden laid down his pen at once and looked over at Simon, his black eye smiling. He stood up then and came closer.

"Let me fetch thee food and drink and tidy up a bit," he said, "and then by words ye can pay me."

So he brought an ewer of water, and washed Simon's face and hands and tended his needs, and brought him porridge and warm milk and a piece of fine white bread spread with honey, and Simon felt like a king. Then he set another pillow behind Simon's head and went back to his stool, but he closed his account book and shoved his quill aside.

"Now, Simon what-ever-other-name-ye-bear, 'tis a law on the land as all men know, against wandering here and there except on pilgrimage or on some stated business, or unless licensed as a beggar or serving as a laborer. The Earl's men come around here now and then, or the Sheriff, casting an eye on all those who have asylum here, and they pick up a man now and then who tells no likely tale. I know not thy business or thy trade—but I know from the snatch I have heard of thy speech that thou art not from hereabouts, and thy hands look too newly blistered to have seen too steady toil, and what's left of thy cloak tells that it was once fine. If I can help in whatever thou art after, that I will, but I must know straight where thou journeys, and why, or from what thou art fleeing. Don't make thy words many, for thou art weak still and fags quickly. But speak me truth, as I truly feel thou wilt."

So Simon looked at him, and the words came bit by bit.

"I come from Colchester, Essex. I was a mercer, and did right well. But I was alone, heart, soul, body, loving naught but myself, seeking naught but my own gain, and yet sick inside, with misery and sin, and the wasting of God's life."

He paused with his eyes on the Warden's face. The Warden nodded, and leaned closer.

"One day, last summer, a man came by. He was a shepherd, and he had a wondrous tale to tell of his city and his master—to the north and then the west it was—a city so full of joy and holy peace, where men dwelt together in love as brothers—and he said it was a city beyond our words to reckon. And he was sent by his master to seek all those lost sheep."

"Who was his master?" whispered the Warden.

"Our Lord Himself, he said it was our Lord Himself."

A golden silence fell on the room, with the firelight and the thin winter sun slanting through the narrow window. The Warden shaded his eye, as if the light were too bright. Simon went on.

"When he had gone I had no rest. I thought that I was going mad, I sought here and there. I roused talk in the town by my crazed ways. And finally, one night, a Poor Priest had died in our parish, and I went to his bier, and found his Bible, and read. And I knew..." he stopped again and watched the Warden's face.

"Go on," whispered the Warden.

"And I knew all I had been taught I could no longer swallow but must spew it forth. So I went about in a black emptiness. And then one day in the tavern I heard a forester talking, and he had met my man, my shepherd, or his brother, and he too, like me, was trapped in his life and could not break free. And then I knew I must go out to seek God for myself, and his city though I died for it, for I was dying at the roots already. And I, who had denied all love, and denied life, have had it put back into my hands in ways I cannot tell. And I am thus far in my search, and pray God I may go still further. Now you know, so do as you like. The Earl's men may come, and I am on no rightful quest in their eyes. But he who has brought me so far will not let loose of me now! I am God's fool now, and he cares for me. As you have cared for me."

The Warden's head was bowed. For a long moment the silence lay on them. Then he raised his head.

"If ever thou reachest that city, wilt thou send back

for me? Once I had a glimpse of it—in my own heart. When I was young, and not so ugly and half-blind. I was taught in the Abbey school, to train for a priest —and I knew the words of the Book, and I could not stomach the life—but I dared not say so—and I ran away, and went to the wars in France—and came back like this, and fit for nothing but to serve the beggars or be one myself. But over the years I have found it a grace to serve the poor for I count no man, neither myself, better than they, and we are all poor in God's sight, those who sleep on silk or on the cobbles of the street. And I will help thee all I can, if thou wilt send back to me, if thou findest that city, God's city, for such there *must be!* Surely Christ came to earth to change this miserable earth, as well as promise the hereafter!"

And he gave a sob, with his hands over his face. Simon, on one elbow, reached out a hand to him.

"Brother, I promise,—unless thou wilt come with me!"

"Nay, that I cannot. I can only go on here. These poor, these filthy poor"—he gestured to the empty pallets by the walls—"who would love them, who would dip their porridge in the mornings, who would quiet them at night? I cannot leave them!"

Simon lay back. The sweat stood on his forehead, and a great pity grew in his heart.

"This city is for them, also. It is for us all. But I

will send back, that I swear," he whispered. And the two clasped hands.

III

The Day Before Christmas

The snow had driven across the land in thick flakes all morning, coating the trees on their north sides, gathering in clumps on the dried weed tops along the road, putting white hoods on the boulders and the stepping stones across the creeks. It was a thick, wetting snow, and Simon felt it driving into each seam and cranny, so he was damp at wrist and neck and ankle, and cold all through. But at noon, when he emerged from the forest, the sun began to shine and the last flakes fell. So he stood at the edge of the wood and looked across the fields to where in its hollow lay the town of Coventry, its roofs white and its spires agleam.

He brushed the snow off a rock and perched on it to rest and eat. He ran over in his mind what he knew of Coventry, a far-famed city. He knew St. Michael's was the largest parish church in England and was even now building a great spire—surely that scaffolded tower on the north. The Abbey was an old one, founded by Leofric, Earl of Chester, and had the richest sanctuary in the kingdom. It was the Duke of Cornwall's city— and famous for its players. And its Bakers' Gild was the largest in the land. It was a rich and lively city, with thick walls and many gates; and from where he perched on his rock he could count two tall spires, besides the one being built, and a host of lesser ones, all sending noon chimes in a medley across the fields.

The cheese and bread left in his sack were soon finished, and pulling his hood partly over his eyes to keep off the glare of the sun on the snow, he rose and slogged on down the track. Where the road was he could scarcely tell except for the bare hedge on one side and a ditch on the other. So he went across the fields, and as the winter sun began to lower and the shadows to lie long, he came wearily to Bablake Gate, and into the city. Hard by the gate was the Guild Church of St. John the Baptist, and the collegiate buildings, with the hospital for poor wayfarers, standing grey and stark. He pushed on, through Gosford Street, and stopped by a town well, Jordan Well, he read on the stone, named for Jordan Stepney, mayor of the city, and perished by the Black Death in 1349. He stood leaning against the stone rim. John Ball, he remembered, had been hidden in a house in this town in the Great Revolt. He looked about him at the houses trim and white, with black timbers, the streets narrow but fairly free of filth, and well-paved.

The stir and sounds of human voices struck him like blows. He felt, as he had felt long ago in Colchester, invisible, until someone brushed against him. The corner where he stood was by Baker Street, and half the city must have been going to and fro for their Christmas sweets. He caught whiffs of anise and clove and bay, and the warm, rich scent of yeast. An alderman in scarlet came past, with his page lugging a wicker pannier. A little boy trotted by with a raisin loaf under his arm, his nose rosy with frost, and a dog at his heels. A Carmelite from Whitefriars came slowly by, in white frock and brown scapulary. Next a draper came past with his apprentice close to his elbow; they carried laden baskets. Three squires came reeling over the cobbles, merry and singing, and two nuns followed, their hands folded and their faces disapproving. They disappeared into the nearest shop.

Simon thought where he should go. He could go back to St. John's Hospice or inquire for Trinity. He could seek shelter there. But it might be dreary past bearing. He still had some coins in his purse from the Warden at St. Edmund's. He would find an inn, pay for a supper and a decent bed and a bit of cheer. It was Christmas after all!

But then his heart smote him. For this was Christmas, and never, never, had it been Christmas before for him. Except when he was a little lad, and clung to his mother's side in the cold church, and wondered at the singing and the lovely shining creche, and felt stirring in him an awe that they all worshiped a baby so small and weak. And he wondered now what the Abbot and the Duke, or the rich draper, felt in their hearts.

And then like a breaking wave the memory of the man descended over him and Simon stood with his fingers clutching the frozen stone of the well. In that city, he wondered, what would they be doing? This was the birthday of their Master and King. And he was sick with longing, his head bent, his eyes blurred.

But it was late, and cold, and darkness coming. He roused himself and went on resolutely, following the crowd toward the center of the town. The square was noisy and gay, and he shouldered his way toward where he saw a sign—a white bull on a black field. It was a large inn, by the looks of it. The leaded windows were warm with light inside. An arched gateway led to the courtyard and the stables. The chimneys were broad and smoking. The wide door opened and shut and a gust of smells came out—roast meat and hot spiced wine and green rushes—and a sound of singing, the clatter of plates, laughter. Simon went nearer. Then he pushed on the door, and went inside. He shut the door and stood with his back against it. The large room was bright with a hearth at either end, and fat beeswax candles set in sconces glowed along the walls. There were settles by the hearth, and long tables, and the room was noisy and crowded. A maid in a green gown came by with a steaming platter of meat and gave him a curious look. She set her platter down on the nearest table and passed by him again, beyond the screens to the kitchens. Then the innkeeper came out, flushed of face, wiping his hands on his apron. He came to Simon and looked him over.

"I seek supper, and a night's lodging," said Simon.

"H'm," said the innkeeper, and he cast his eye about the room. " 'Tis a more humble place ye seek. Try the White Cock, on Crooked Lane."

"But it is late, and darkening, and I a stranger," said Simon, softly. "I must find shelter before curfew."

The door opened behind Simon, and three men swept in—a merchant, and his clerk, and his boy. The merchant wore a cloak with an ermine border and scarlet hose. The innkeeper rubbed his hands.

"To the kitchen," he hissed at Simon, and went forward to his new guests. Simon slipped behind the screens and into the warm kitchen. The maid in the green gown was basting a fowl. She glanced up, and motioned him to a bench near the hearth. Simon sat and watched while she and two boys flitted in and out with food and drink. At length the innkeeper came back. He cut a wedge from a hot pie and thrust it on a trencher and fetched a flagon of ale, and set both before Simon.

"Eat," he said, gruffly. "There is no bed here left—

but ye can stay in the stable if ye've a mind to. Mayhap ye'll see the beasts kneel at midnight—'tis Holy Eve— or hear them talk." He laughed. "I once knew a shepherd who swore such tales were true. Perhaps when the world was young!" and he hurried on.

Simon ate in silence and exhaustion. Weariness was his companion, he thought, and loneliness his continuing bondage. The maid came back. He had finished his food, and now he laid down a coin for it, and rose.

"Which way the stable?" he asked.

She jerked her thumb toward a door in the far wall. He walked over and opened it, going out into the courtyard. He stood for a moment in the dark and cold, until the starlight grew, and then he saw the stables on the left. He went slowly across the flagstones and opened the wide stable door on its old creaking hinges, and stepped inside, carefully pulling the door to behind him.

What it was that came to him then he could not have told. But the world changed. He stood in the breathing dark and smelled the sour-sweet stable smell, and a sudden joy surged over him.

"It was here the Lord was born!" he whispered. Not in the warm glowing inn, not in the gleaming sanctuary, not in the great Abbey, not in the tidy houses. Here, in a miserable stable!

Simon stood still, and his heart thudded. Little by little he began to see around him, by the faint star-

light from the narrow window. The horses stamped
in their stalls, and overhead a pigeon cooed and re-
settled herself. On the right he saw a dim white shape
lying on the straw, and he moved that way. It was
a cow, and over the edge of her stall a donkey drooped
his head; his big ears dipped toward Simon, who put
out a hand and scratched him between the eyes. The
cow was warm and quiet, and Simon sank into the
straw beside her. He leaned against the wall and
stared before him into the faint light. The world was
new-made, and he almost feared to touch it.

He had never thought, truly, of to whom he owed
his loyalty, to whom he gave fealty—yet now he knew.
It was to a man like himself, poor and despised, yet
truly God; one to whom all kings must bow. Yet all
poor men, who knelt to so many, must also kneel to
him in their hearts, who came as poor as they, and
who died despised. But he came and he died that he
might always walk with them, in all things, and that
they might share out of God's great mercy, in this
miracle of love, past all understanding. And what he
called men out from—those poor fishermen and mend-
ers of nets—he still called men from, and just as they
then were his, so he, Simon, could be his. And not
alone. But at his Master's feet. Always. And he could
serve him now—in this instant—as the Man served
him, as his City served him. He, Simon, could be
Christ's fool, his least servant—now, in this instant, in

a stable in Coventry. And he wanted to sing with joy, that Christ was born and had come to him. So he sat in the breathing dark of the stable, and listened to the bells, and worshiped the Babe. And after a long while he lay against the warm cow and slept.

IV

January 21

He was traveling through the Malvern Hills on the 20th day of January, rising before dawn from the shelter of an empty forester's hut. He had crossed the Severn below Worcester, after staying in the town long enough to earn bread and lodging by copying accounts for a mercer. On the night of the 20th he sheltered in an abandoned hermitage. In the morning it was bitter cold; the trees, each separate dead grass stem, each brown frond of bracken silver with hoar; and by a little stream he crossed, the mist had frozen like jeweled ferns along the bank. As he went on and the sun rose higher the hoar melted and dripped, the dazzle vanished little by little, and the world turned brown again. He sang as he went, a wordless jumbled tune, but full of praise anyway, and he laughed at himself.

He came down out of the hills in the afternoon, and found the road to the bridge over Leadon River, and saw in the distance the huddled cottages of the village of Dymock. He set off that way, hoping for shelter, and because it looked a simple place, unwalled and castleless.

By the bridge some small boys were playing at staves. He heard their shouts as he came near, and the sound of hard thwacks, and a sudden crying; then an angry clamor broke out.

When Simon appeared amongst them they all fell back, silent, except the little boy on the ground who held his leg and continued to raise a howl. Simon looked at each grubby face, each heaving chest, and last he looked at the boy on the ground, who suddenly ceased howling and got up, wiping his nose on his sleeve. Simon smiled.

"None the worse?" he queried, and the boy shook his head.

"A game's a game," said Simon. "Best fling these in the river"—pointing to the staves—"if they bring anger instead of pleasure."

The biggest lad picked up the staves.

" 'Tis nearly sundown, and we'd best be going home, anyway," he said. "Yonder is our village, and we could take ye the shortest way, across the fields, if that is where you are set to go. There is a hostel by the church for travelers, and many a hearth would give ye shelter."

So Simon fell in with them, and they clattered over the wooden bridge, and went off across the wet meadows. They whistled to their dogs, who came one by one to sniff at Simon and wag their tails at him. They chattered like starlings in a bush about fishing, falcons, and the skill of making rushlights. Only the little boy who had cried was silent, and he stayed by Simon's side, and after a bit took Simon's hand. So they came into the village, and one by one the boys turned off home, till none were left but Simon and the little boy, and then they stood by the hostel. It was brown and bleak, and Simon looked at it with a sinking heart. The little boy tugged at his hand.

"It is only a mean house, where I live, but..."

"I slept last night in an empty, bare hut," said Simon, looking down at him. "What would thy mother say, if thee brought me home?"

"We are poor," whispered the little boy, "and she is sad."

"Then mayhap I can help make her merrier," said Simon, "and I would like much to see thy house."

"But that is not all. I have a little sister, and she can't see. And my father..."

"Yes?"

"He goes into great rages," and the little boy shivered.

"Come," said Simon. "Show me the way." So they set off down the road again, and at the farthest cottage, in a ruined brown garden, they turned in.

The girl who rose from beside the fire was tall and slender; her face was pale and tired, and her hands red with chapping. She looked at her boy, and then at the strange man.

"He stopped with us where we were playing, Mother, and I brought him home. He was going to stay at the hostel, but it looked so comfortless."

She smiled a little wryly.

"Nay, Dickon, any stranger is welcome here, though there be little comfort here also—"

"Then may he stay?"

"Lady," broke in Simon, "this lad would not let me go. I will be no trouble, but also do what I can to fetch and carry, or mend what the lad is still too small to mend for thee, and can sleep in the shed I saw outside, gladly."

The girl looked at him then, and her tired face softened.

"First sit and rest. And Dickon, fetch our guest cider from the shed, and clean his shoes and thy own clogs, and fetch in a bit of wood." She pulled out a stool for Simon. "And go about it softly, for Elspeth sleeps."

Simon sat, and let his weariness thaw out by the fire. Dickon vanished outside. The mother pulled oatcakes from the fire, and stirred a kettle of cabbages and curds. Then she stooped over a pallet that lay beneath the settle. On it was curled a golden-haired little girl.

"The boy said he had a little sister," Simon spoke softly.

"Yes," said the mother, and sighed.

"I lost my little lass, long ago. She was golden-haired also."

The mother ran her fingers softly over the child's head.

"This little one is blind," she whispered, "and perhaps better off where thy little one has gone. The world is hard and coldhearted to such as she."

"Nay," replied Simon, "not everywhere."

The woman looked up. "I could give her to the Sisters to raise...but God sent her to me, and I love her more than my own life."

Then Dickon came in and set a mug of cider by Simon, and stooped to take his boots to clean. Simon made him sit instead, and rolled down the hose on his right leg. There was a great bruise on his shin, from the stave blow. Simon slipped his hand under Dickon's chin and tipped up his face.

"Thee cried because it hurt!"

Dickon nodded dumbly.

"Then why did thee stop howling?"

"Because...because it did not hurt enough to spoil all, and for me to lie there in my own misery! And thee stood there and looked at me."

Then they both laughed aloud, and the little girl

on the pallet woke, and sat up, turning misty eyes
their way.

"Now, Elspeth is awakened by our noise, lad. And
I must make amends for it. Fetch me a bit of grease
and a rag, and I'll fix thy leg, and then maybe I can
search my memory for a tale that might please a
little girl, though such a little one as that needs a
very little tale."

Dickon fetched as he was bid. The mother brought
the little girl out, and laid her hand in Simon's. She
had a round, rosy little face and Simon drew her
close. She reached up her free hand and felt his
beard and nose and eyes, and last reached around to
pull at his ear. He crowed like a cock, and she drew
back her hand, then suddenly sensed the jest, and
gently tugged his ear again, and again he crowed. The
little girl laughed a merry laugh and tried the other
ear. That time a hen cackled. The mother stood and
watched the game, her face alight, and Dickon, waiting
to have his leg mended, began to quack. So Elspeth
tried his ears, but soon came back to Simon, and
perched on his lap, and there stayed while he spooned
her supper into her, and gave her a mug of barley
water. At last, after they had all had a merry supper,
she went to sleep on his shoulder, and he laid her
down, and covered her crumpled blue gown gently
with a little quilt. The mother lit her tallow candle
and set it on the table. Dickon's head was nodding,

and she sent him to his bed. Simon sat by the fire shaping a new leg for a broken stool. The mother brought her mending to the table, but the candle light was too feeble. She thrust her needle into the patched garment, put it aside, and stared into the flames. Then she looked at Simon.

"Art on a long journey? Art going home?" she asked.

He peeled off another curl of wood and tossed it into the fire. He smiled faintly.

"Lady, I may be nearing journey's end. I travel out of exile, home."

"Ever since Dickon brought thee, I meant to ask. He is a shy and wary lad, and for him to bring a stranger in puzzled me. But where was thy exile, and for why? If thou canst tell me. And where is thy city to which thee returneth?"

Simon's hands were at rest and his face shone.

"I was in exile as all men are in exile, out of a proud and stubborn loneliness, out of a lovelessness, and a cold heart, and unbelieving." He shook his head a bit as if to drive those memories away. "And then my brother came to me, though I did not know him, and he called me home, and proclaimed my true master, and I had no peace until I had set forth. And so I travel homewards, though I have never seen that city—yet will I know it, and its fair meadows are even now green with winter wheat before my eyes, and I hear its children singing in the streets, and its quiet bell proclaiming God's love."

The mother's hands were white as she gripped the table edge and leaned toward him.

"Where is that city?" she whispered.

"North of here, somewhere over the mountains. That is all I know."

"Who is the Lord of that city?"

"Jesus, son of Mary, he is Lord of that city, and none other."

There was no sound except the snap of the flames and the breathing of the children. The room was golden in the firelight. And then the mother put down her head and began to weep.

"Would I could go with thee," she wept, "but I cannot, I cannot. My man, I cannot leave him. He goes off for days, raving, in the forest, and comes back sick and half-starved, weak and helpless. He was a clerk, but with our marriage ruined all, and the Abbey turned him off. Yonder are his pens and parchment. The loveliest letters he could do—all gold and blue scrolls, with peacocks and unicorns and pome-granates. So he went as a common laborer to earn our bread—but after Elspeth came he blamed him-self for her affliction, and went mad, in these fits of raving when I cannot hold him here, and cannot follow. And no one can help. But surely in thy city there is forgiveness, and peace, and life for a little blind inno-cent, and a Master to be loved beyond measure!"

"Lady, my sister," said Simon, softly, "have no fear. My city is thy city also. And when I find it, I shall come back for thee, and for thine."

She raised her head and looked at him then, and the color came to her cheeks.

"Canst find thy way here again?" she asked, half-believing.

"Bring me parchment, and ink and quill," said Simon. So she rose and brought it, blowing the dust away from the roll, and shaking the ink in its little jar. With his knife he cut a piece from the parchment. Then he dipped the quill, and laboriously began to write. The mother stood watching him, her hands clasped to her heart. He looked up at her.

"Thy name?" he asked.

"Julian, of Dymock, by Leadon River. And my man, he is Stephen."

Simon wrote it down, and wrote some more. Then he laid aside the quill and put the piece of parchment in the wallet on his belt, fastening it securely. Then he rose and faced her.

"Dost thou believe me?"

"Yea, and even now I serve him in my heart."

"Then tomorrow I must journey on, but first sleep, if I may." And he moved toward the door. Julian gathered up a bearskin from the corner and gave it to him, and Simon went out into the night, to sleep in the shed.

193

V

February 15

He had crossed the River Wye many days before, traveling slowly now, for the way was hard and he was weary to the bone. The way led up, and was rocky and steep, then down into shallow valleys where no man dwelt, then up again into the craggy hills. Here lived the golden eagle; and the shy little stoat, in its winter dress, who crouched on its ledge against the snow and watched him pass. He saw the track of deer and hare, and little prints of birds. He ate sparingly of what was in his wallet, and sucked snow when he was thirsty, and he pushed on, keeping the sun on his left. He was never warm, and always hungry, and in pain, but he did not know it, and went on, unheeding.

There came a day of thaw, and warm sun. The earth smelt new, and the ferns in the hollows were green and fresh. A grey bird with a rosy breast and bright black eye watched him as he ate his hard bread by a little stream and scooped water in his palm. Simon sang to it, and threw it crumbs, and laughed, and felt fresh courage. He was in a little valley, before him a steep cliff, with a trace of a path going up its face.

And as he sat there resting and drinking in the silence, he heard a bell.

It sounded muted and far, yet very clear, and after a time ceased. Simon sat as if in a spell, his heart thudding. And then he stood up. On either side as far as he could see the cliff rose. Before him was that trace of path, the only way that he could see. So he began to climb.

He knew that others had been there before him, for here and there a step seemed hewn out of the rock, or a root that served as a handhold was worn and smooth. And halfway up he found the remains of a fire on a broad ledge, where someone had rested and warmed himself. Simon also rested there, and then looked back across the little valley, to the hills beyond that he had climbed. Then he turned to go upward again, and it was there, in a little green hollow, that he found it.

It was a blue flower. It grew all alone; it was cupped like a buttercup, blue-veined gold in the center, with three black stamens tipped with gold. He stared at it, sobbing with joy. And then with trembling fingers he reached out and plucked it very gently. He cupped it in his hands as if it were the fairest jewel. And then he looked up at the cliff, and the steep path. He tucked the flower into his tunic, and began to climb, more quickly now, his breath coming in gasps, his hands scratched, the sweat running into his eyes, his arms aching.

He climbed up, and up, never looking forward or back, but simply at the next foothold, the next tree or shrub to clutch. He passed more little green protected hollows, where the blue flowers grew, and he sobbed with joy and climbed higher. When he reached the top he hardly knew it, but suddenly found himself on a level, where there were large rocks and thick green laurel bushes, and the path ran straight before him. He staggered and caught himself against a rock, the breath rasping in his throat, and then he went on, straight through the bushes, and out into the sun.

There he stood in a dazzle. He stood at the edge of a sloping meadow, and before him there fell away a fair valley, with the sun a-shimmer over it, the fields green with winter wheat, the near pasture dotted with sheep. Below there was the clustered village, and as he stood, a solitary figure against the forest edge, the bell began to peal, and out of the village figures began to run, streaming out to meet him. A shepherd in the nearest field turned, and saw him, and broke into a stride his way.

And then Simon knew. Joy, like a great golden flower, grew and grew within his breast. The pain of it swelled and swelled and finally shattered. The valley opened out, broader and broader, into a golden kingdom, with many bells, and a vast host hastening out to welcome him. And he reached out his hands and cried, "Master! I have come!"

The shepherd was the first to reach him. He lay with his back against a rock, and his open eyes fixed on the village below, in his hands a blue flower. The shepherd gently closed his eyes, and the shepherd's dog stood with head down, and his tail drooping and still. The shepherd was bearded and brown-visaged, with blue eyes and lashes like starpoints. When his brothers came up and stood in a silent circle he said quietly, "I found him in Colchester, many months ago. I felt someday I would set eyes on his face again. Truly he has come home."

They took up a trestle, and the shepherd flung his cloak over it, and on this they laid Simon, and carried him down into the village. They made his bier in a small room set with greens and candles, and they placed a cluster of blue flowers in his hands. And one by one they came to look on his face, in sorrow and yet in joy that in death they were not divided. And the children sang in the road outside. And all night, in twos, his brothers watched by his side.

And in the morning, just after dawn, while they were digging his grave, the shepherd set forth. He went across the fields and up the sloping meadow, and disappeared into the forest edge along the path. In his wallet he carried Simon's parchment and on it was written:

To be Gathered:
Julian, and her man Stephen,
with their children, of
Dymock, near Leadon River

The Warden,
St. Edmund's Hospice,
Leicester,

An unnamed forester,
from near Cantebrege,
with a wife named Nan.
Gillian, a little lass,
of Duck Lane
Colchester.

oh seek!

Oh seek! while the hills remain.
God calls, though daylight fails,
the cruel, the pitiful, the proud,
the weak, the brave, the covetous,
the faltering, the wise, the poor,
the kings, the lepers, and the crowd.

Struck through with death, we hold the seed;
life springs, though our pale roots are dry;
though heaven never seemed so high
God stoops, to touch our need.

And all the ages fall away;
eyes meet, and shoulders touch at last;
Christ waits, and gathers in His day
the present, future, and the past.
Hallelujah! Amen.

Behold That Star: A Christmas Anthology. Fifteen stories from many lands, illustrated by Maria Arnold Maendel. Authors include B.J. Chute, Elizabeth Goudge, Selma Lagerlöf, and Ruth Sawyer. 6¼ × 8½ in., 364 pages, cloth.

Inner Land: A Guide into the Heart and Soul of the Bible by Eberhard Arnold. Available in five volumes: 1 The Inner Life, 2 The Struggle of the Conscience, 3 The Experience of God and His Peace, 4 Light and Fire and the Holy Spirit, 5 The Living Word. 5 × 7½ in., each volume about 100 pages, cloth. Also available in one volume, 588 pages, cloth.

Salt and Light: Talks and Writings on the Sermon on the Mount by Eberhard Arnold. 4¼ × 7 in., 338 pages, paper; 5 × 7½ in., 344 pages, cloth.

The Early Christians after the Death of the Apostles by Eberhard Arnold. An unusual collection of early Christian sources covering the period A.D. 70 to 180. 350 texts including sayings of Jesus. It contains many texts so far inaccessible to the general reader, and gives a comprehensive and challenging insight into the life and faith of the early Christians in a hostile, pagan environment. 6½ × 9 in., 484 pages, cloth.

Torches Together: The Beginning and Early Years of the Bruderhof Communities by Emmy Arnold. 6 × 8 in., 240 pages, paper; 6¼ × 8¼ in., 240 pages, cloth.

Seeking for the Kingdom of God: Origins of the Bruderhof Communities by Eberhard and Emmy Arnold. 6¼ × 8¼ in., 304 pages, cloth.

In the Image of God: Marriage and Chastity in Christian Life by Heini Arnold. "This book was put together in a special effort to fight the corrupting impurity in the world today. It is terrible to see how millions of young people are misled by what is made of sex today in magazines and newspapers, radio and television. I felt an urge to write something about the area of sex experienced with God or without God. The Church, wherever it truly lives, has to fight for purity that comes from God." Heini Arnold. 4¼ × 7 in., 188 pages, paper.

Love and Marriage in the Spirit by Eberhard Arnold. In these talks and essays on the nature of man, and of woman, and on true marriage in the uniting power of God's love, Eberhard Arnold addressed himself to what he considered one of the main problems of young people. 5¼ × 7½ in., 260 pages, cloth.

When the Time Was Fulfilled: On Advent and Christmas. Talks and writings by Eberhard Arnold, Christoph Blumhardt, Alfred Delp, and others. 5½ × 7½ in., 254 pages, cloth.

Children's Education in Community: The Basis of Bruderhof Education by Eberhard Arnold. 5 × 7¼ in., 68 pages, paper.

Songs of Light: The Bruderhof Songbook. Compiled and edited by the Hutterian Society of Brothers from Eberhard Arnold and many other sources. Music editor: Marlys Swinger; art editor: Gillian Barth. 376 songs. The songs in this major Plough work are arranged in three broad sections: General, Christmas, and Easter, consisting of several subsections each introduced by an original pen-and-ink drawing. Indexes of English first lines and titles, of German first lines and titles, and of topics make it a very usable book. 6 × 9 in., 560 pages, cloth.

Write for a complete listing of Plough books.

Names and addresses of the communities of the Hutterian Society of Brothers:

Woodcrest, Rifton, New York 12471
New Meadow Run, Farmington, Pennsylvania 15437
Deer Spring, Norfolk, Connecticut 06058
Darvell, Robertsbridge, Sussex, England TN32 5DR